SPALDING HIGH SCHOOL MEDIA CENTER

DELETED

A Time for Dancing

A Time for Dancing

A Novel by

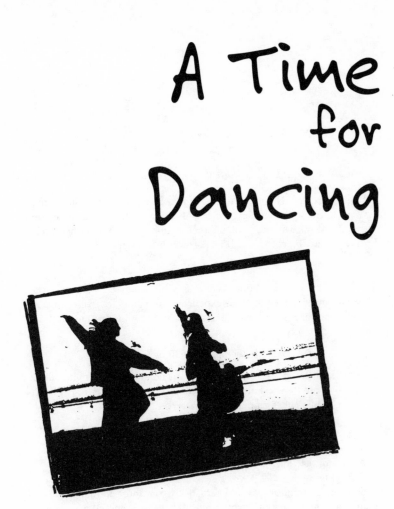

Davida Wills Hurwin

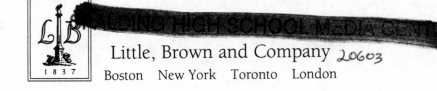

Little, Brown and Company

Boston New York Toronto London

First Edition

Library of Congress Cataloging-in-Publication Data

Hurwin, Davida Wills.
A time for dancing / a novel by Davida Wills Hurwin. — 1st ed.
p. cm.
Summary: Seventeen-year-old best friends Samantha and Juliana tell their stories in alternating chapters after Juliana is diagnosed with cancer.
ISBN 0-316-38351-1
[1. Cancer — Patients — Fiction. 2. Friendship — Fiction. 3. Death — Fiction. 4. Grief — Fiction. 5. [Fic]] I. Title.
PZ7.H95735Ti 1995 95-7169

10 9 8 7 6 5 4 3

MV-NY

Published simultaneously in Canada by Little, Brown & Company (Canada) Limited

Printed in the United States of America

For
Mama and Daddy
and Frazier and Gene

Love and Thanks
to
Nigel McKeand
Mary Ann Bleier
Jean Campbell
Lynn Pleshette and Eric Feig
Bonnie Nadell
Jackie Horne
and to my mentor and friend,
Carol Evan McKeand

A Time for Dancing

Part One

Julie

"Ten."

"You're crazy. Four. *Maybe.*"

"Ten. No doubt."

"Who are *you* looking at?"

"Black pants, black shirt, black hair. By the couch."

"Shut up. He's a twit."

"*I* like him."

"Sam . . ."

"I'm going to go meet him."

"You are not."

"Watch me."

"Samantha. Don't you dare leave me here."

"I will."

"Fine. What if Jack comes?"

"You'll cope."

"Sam!"

"Jules!"

I looked over at my best friend, my Samantha Jefferson Russell the First, then at the dweeb she was lusting for, and back again. She had her lips pressed together and that try-and-stop-me look in her eyes, so I shrugged and told her, "Go ahead." No one ever kept Sam from anything she really wanted to do. All you got from trying was a headache. She could outlast any kind of opposition, and once she made up her mind, you might as well forget arguing. Her stubbornness made me crazy, but I loved her for it. I always knew exactly who she was, and I understood her, like she understood me. We were connected, best friends for more than half our lives, two parts of the same being.

I shook my head and smiled as she glided across the room. Pale skin, thick white-blond hair, huge blue eyes; she was like a colt, skinny and long-legged and sort of unfinished-looking, but perfect. The black-haired guy saw her coming and tried to act cool, but the poor boy didn't have a chance. I chuckled. This party was going to be fine.

Pushing my hair back, I snuck a peek at the reflection in my glass and smiled. I'm nowhere near Sam when it comes to beautiful, but basically, I'm okay. My hair is the kind of black that has a touch of reddish brown in it, my skin is olive, and my eyes are big and dark, dark brown (Sam calls them chocolate eyes). We're exactly the same, in height and build, and exactly opposite in color. Light and Dark, Day and Night, Sun and Moon. Together, we're awesome.

Sitting back, I took a look around. Brooke had been giving her thank-God-it's-almost-summer parties on Memorial Day weekend every year since seventh grade, at her parents' "getaway" house on Mount Tamalpais. This would be the next-to-last one, since we were going to be seniors. I couldn't believe it. So much had already passed, and so much more was just waiting to happen. Where would we all be in two years? Me: someplace with Sam, I guessed, college or dancing — or both. It was almost too much to consider. Everything was beginning and at this one little moment, I felt ready for it all. I watched the people and appreciated the house — a perfect place to contemplate life. One whole wall was sliding glass, with a deck suspended over the cliffs and the ocean below. There were no outside lights, only the night and the stars and a feeling of endlessness.

Just then, I heard a too-familiar voice. Jack had managed to sneak in and was across the room by the piano, talking to Brooke and a few other girls. My stomach contracted. I took a deep breath. Jack and I had been together almost eight months. Three weeks ago, he'd broken it off — with no explanation except "I guess I just need some space." After I'd cried for a week, I started planning how I would get him back. I'd avoided talking to him at school but made sure he'd seen me having fun and looking wonderful. I knew tonight would be my chance to connect. Sam thought I was crazy, but Sam was in the corner with her dark boy, not paying a bit of attention to me. I took a long sip of my drink and got myself ready.

He looked over. Like Sam, he was my physical opposite, blond and fair, about six feet tall, with hazel-green eyes and a mouth that was almost but not quite too big for the rest of his face. Not actually good-looking, but definitely sexy. Plus he was an artist, a good one. I smiled. He smiled back and started toward me. I glanced to see if Sam was watching; then I noticed he was holding this girl's hand. Had been holding it as he talked to Brooke. Continued to hold it as he led her over toward me. Behind them, Brooke made a helpless face, and I realized she'd been trying to keep him away. I blinked and he was there, looking down at me. He put his arm around the girl and drew her close.

"Julie — this is Rachael. We're, uh, kind of going out now, and I sort of wanted you to hear it from me."

I looked down for a minute. It took every single piece of determination I had not to throw up. I don't know how I did it, but I made myself not blush. I forced my face to stop twitching. I ordered my eyes not to cry, and I lowered my drink to my lap so they wouldn't see my hand was shaking. When I looked back up, smiling, unconcerned, even my voice was easy, natural — maybe just a touch condescending.

"It's nice to meet you, Rachael. Do you go to school around here?"

Rachael smiled a sly smile. She was in fact a sly-looking girl, almost as tall as Jack and bony, with a horse face and long scary fingers that ended in red-enameled claws. She had bleached her hair, and it hung around her zombie face in clumps, with a streak of burgundy down the side. Not Jack's type of girl. At all.

"I go to Tam, Julie." She smirked. "In fact, we have P.E. together."

"Oh." I almost lost it. "I guess I never noticed."

"Well, I've been there. Jack and I do art together."

"Really. That's great. Jack's always liked art."

"Probably more than you know."

Then silence. The noise of the party intruded as Jack stood there with this stupid grin, clueless to what a bitch this freak was being. Knowing that if I said one more word, I'd be sorry for it in the morning, I yawned instead. I hate people to see when I'm upset or vulnerable. I glanced over at Sam, but no help there — she was dancing with her boy and didn't even see me. Jack hadn't let go of Rachael, and all of a sudden, things were a lot clearer.

This was no three-week relationship. How stupid could I be? All that time, being there for him after his father had died, telling people how much he loved me. I felt a little dizzy. Did everybody else already know about her? Were they laughing behind my back? Feeling sorry for me? I felt myself starting to panic.

"Gotta go," I said, surprisingly nonchalant, then stood up and kissed Jack dead on the lips, much longer than a friend should. "Love you." I managed to turn away just as the tears hit.

Just that second, Sam happened to look over and was by my side in a flash, her new boy close behind. Looking past me to Jack and Rachael, she stared blatantly, then gave me such a look of disgust I burst out laughing. How could I even have worried about "that"? her expression asked. I shrugged in reply, already feeling better. Her new boy just looked confused, and after she introduced us, she sent him off for a drink. Then she dragged me into the other room.

"We're out of here," she announced. "Get your stuff."

"But —," I protested.

"Look, you don't need this. We're going, okay?"

"What about what's-his-name?"

She made a face at me and I giggled.

"So you were right, for once. Okay? Now get your stuff. We'll go down to the beach."

We found Brooke, thanked her, assured her I was doing okay, and made our exit just before the dark-haired boy came back with drinks. From behind the door, Sam pointed and shook her head as he stupidly looked around for us. I giggled again, feeling fine, until we came out of the house and saw Rachael and Jack up on the deck, kissing and groping. I couldn't help staring, and the tears came for real. Sam grabbed my hand and pulled me away.

"Stop it."

"I'm trying. . . ."

"Try harder."

"I hate this," I told her as I turned back for another look. She whipped me back around and kept me moving toward the car.

"I need to look."

"No, you don't." She pulled me harder. "Come on. Do you want them to see you crying?"

I shook my head. Sam reached behind and goosed me, and I jumped and shrieked, loud enough to attract Jack's attention. As he and Rachael turned to look, we piled into Sam's car, laughing and being silly.

"That's how you do it," she told me, smiling.

I tried to smile back. I couldn't.

"Stop stressing, woman. You're gonna be fine."

I managed a nod, but the way I was feeling inside, I wasn't so sure.

Sam

I should've known the party would be a disaster. The whole day had sucked. Thanks to my mom, who spent an entire two hours hogging the bathroom, I didn't finish my shower until fifteen minutes after I was supposed to pick up Jules. Trying to hurry, I cut my leg shaving, and of course it wouldn't stop bleeding, even with toilet paper stuck to it. And of course I had a huge zit sitting on my chin, waiting to explode. Nothing I could do about that, either. I wrapped a towel around my hair, slipped on my bathrobe, and went to get dressed. I called Jules to tell her not to stress, and then the doorbell rang.

"Shit!" my mom yelled from her room. "Get that for me, would you?"

"I can't," I called back. "You get it."

"Honey, it's Bruce."

"Mother, I'm late."

It rang again.

"Just answer the stupid door, Samantha. Two seconds. I'll be right out."

I made a face in her direction and went to the door. Bruce was the new boyfriend, a middle-aged wanna-be cool guy with no hair on the top of his head. He'd been "dating" my mom for almost three months and thought I didn't know they were sleeping together. He was nice enough, I guess, but never had a clue what to say to me. I opened the door and almost laughed in his face. He was wearing tight black Levis and a paisley shirt. He looked like a character from *Saturday Night Live.*

"Hey, hey, hey, how are you, little lady?"

"Fine, thanks. Mom'll be right out."

"Getting ready for that big date, huh? Huh?"

"No, not really."

"Too bad. As pretty as you are, the boys should be flocking." He flashed a huge grin and patted my shoulder. "Well, don't worry about it. You'll have a boyfriend before you know it."

I gave him a look. "That's a really sexist thing to say," I told him. "I mean, what if I was a lesbian or something? What if I didn't even want a boyfriend?"

He blinked a couple of times, and his mouth opened and closed. He pretended he hadn't heard me. He grinned a few seconds longer, then nodded and patted me again.

"Well, I'll just make myself at home. Jackie's almost ready?"

"That's what she said."

"I'll be right there, honey," my mom sang from her room. I took the opportunity to exit.

Fifteen minutes later, dressed and made up, I was looking for my car keys when my mom marched into my room. She was definitely not happy.

"What is so hard about being nice to my friends?" she demanded. "I am always nice to yours."

"What are you talking about?"

"Bruce told me what you said." She shook her head at me. "What are you trying to prove?"

"Do we have to do this now? I'm late."

"You're not going anywhere until I get an answer."

"I was teasing, okay? What's the big deal? He can't take a joke?"

"Rudeness is not funny."

"Oh. But it's okay if he asks me all about my personal life."

"Don't get smart with me, young lady. You know what I'm talking about. And you are really pissing me off."

"So what else is new?" I said under my breath.

"Look, Samantha. This is the first boyfriend I've had that I really care about. It would be nice if you could manage not to be a complete ass. Especially if you want to continue driving that car. Are we clear?"

I blinked and looked away.

"Are we clear?"

"Yes."

"Good. We're leaving now. Don't get home too late."

"I won't."

"Is Julie spending the night?"

"I guess."

"I may stay over at Bruce's."

"Okay."

"Call me if you need anything."

"Okay."

She paused and sighed. "Look, Sammie, think about what I said, all right?"

"Yeah."

"I'm not trying to be mean. You just need to learn a little common courtesy."

"Okay. Fine."

"And Bruce really likes you, honey."

I didn't speak. She kissed me on the forehead and sailed out, leaving her perfume all over my room and this big lump of anger inside me. A second later she was laughing with Bruce. I stayed still on my bed and waited. When I heard his Jag pull away, I found my car keys, grabbed a Doors tape, and got in my Jeep. Blasting it all the way to Jules's house, I sang along and started to feel more in control. Jules came out, looking wonderful, as usual, and by the time we made our entrance to Brooke's party, I felt great.

Then, of course, Jack showed up with The Freak. I would have killed him right there, in front of everybody. Except that Jules wouldn't have liked it. And she had started to crash.

So I took her out of that party, past Jack and his bitch, and into my car. She sat staring out the front window as we backed out onto the road and started down the mountain to the beach. I drove slowly and stopped at the last curve before you wind down to the water. It was a clear night, and only a few cars passed us going the other way.

"You okay?" I asked Jules. She nodded without looking at me. "We can go back to my house any time you want. Mother Dear is with the boyfriend." She shook her head and tried to keep herself from crying again. I started down to Stinson Beach.

We parked on a side road, grabbed a blanket from my trunk, and went down by the private paths. Each beach is its own area, bounded by cliffs, with trees that grow right down to the sand line. The actual park is closed at night, but you can walk over to it through the yards of the houses people own along the beach. If you don't make too much noise or light a fire, no one bothers you. The night was icy cold, with a bright full moon in the sky and on the water. Lights from the beach houses made it feel friendly and safe. We found a cozy nook in a cluster of rocks and sat down.

The sound of the ocean reached out, and Jules responded. I knew she would. She's a Scorpio, a water sign, and the best way to get her to mellow out is to take her to the ocean. They talk. I'm serious. She sat quietly and listened to the waves crashing and retreating. Whatever they were saying, she needed to hear. Her shoulders relaxed, her hands got still, and a couple of tears slid down her face. She wiped them away and sighed — the slow, long releasing kind.

"I hate this," she said, still looking at the ocean.

"I know."

"I feel stupid."

"Yeah." I touched her hand, but she moved it away. She turned and stared at me.

"Did you know he was with her?"

I shook my head. Her eyes checked my face.

"Promise?"

I looked away. "Well, I kinda knew. I wasn't sure."

She glared at me.

"I saw them hanging out after school last week. Remember? I told you about it."

"No, you didn't."

"Yes, I did. In the car, on the way back from dance."

"Well, I didn't hear you. Otherwise I wouldn't have gone to the stupid party."

We sat a moment.

"Do you think he was, you know . . . *with* her . . . at the same time we were together?"

"Absolutely not." She stared at me, and I stared right back.

Finally she turned back to the ocean and listened awhile. This time when I put my hand on hers, she didn't move. From somewhere way off down the beach, two people started laughing. Jules sighed and spoke.

"I thought for sure we'd get back together."

"Yeah, I know."

"Things just don't end like this. People don't just drop out of each other's lives."

I thought of my dad but kept my mouth shut.

"What am I supposed to do now?" she asked.

"Ignore him. Then forget him."

"I can't."

"Sure you can. I do it all the time."

"Well, I'm not like you."

"Jules, he's not worth it."

She shot me a look. "You always say that."

"Because it's true. He doesn't deserve you."

"Too bad for me, then, because I love him."

"I don't think so. I think you love the idea of him."

"Thanks so much for your support." She pulled her hand away.

"What do you want me to say? He's a manipulator."

"He is not."

"Jules, he does nothing but take. You give; he takes. He's done it since the beginning."

"Don't start."

"Why? I'm right."

"You just don't like him."

"How'd you guess?"

"You don't understand. He's not like you think. He's got a whole other side. . . ."

"Uh-huh."

"He does."

"Sure, I believe that. Not."

Jules's face clouded, and her voice turned low and scary. "You weren't there when his dad died. You didn't sit with him and hold him and not know what to do. You didn't watch him cry and cry and cry till he couldn't cry anymore. So don't tell me you understand, okay?" She sighed. "Why are you being so mean?"

We stared at each other, and I turned away first. Jules started crying again, very softly. She finally looked away from me and back to the sea. Her beautiful face was dark and sad. Just hours ago, we'd been laughing and planning our entrance to Brooke's party. She'd made me completely forget the thing with my mom. What was I doing? This was my best friend, my One and Only.

"I'm sorry, Jules."

She didn't respond.

"I just hate to see you so unhappy."

Still no answer. She wouldn't look at me.

I sat for a minute, then plopped myself down in front of her, grabbed her legs, and groveled in a silly little girl's voice, "Oh please, oh please, oh please . . . don't be mad. It's not my fault he's being a jerk."

"Stop." She almost smiled.

"I'll kiss your feet. . . ." I lunged for them. She giggled. "Sam . . . stop!"

"I'll try and like him."

She threw me a look.

"I will, I promise . . . just don't be mad at me, okay?"

"Don't be stupid. I'm not mad at you."

"Could've fooled me."

"I know. I'm sorry. I'm probably overreacting. I've got a virus, or cold, or something. . . . It's making me feel off."

I sat back up. "I bet it's stress."

"It could be. Anyway, I'm not myself."

I nodded, and she sighed. "But I really do love him, Sam. I really really do."

"Come on," I said, not knowing what else to do. I stood up and held out a hand for Jules. "Let's walk."

We left our shoes on the blanket and went down by the water, walking toward the moon and yelping when the icy surf touched our toes. I still wanted to kill Jack, but more important was making Jules feel better.

"Hey . . . ," I said, "do you think we'll get to do 'The Little Girls' Dance'? If it's ready?"

"For the Showcase?"

"No, stupid, for my mother's wedding." I pushed her. "Of course for the Showcase."

"How do I know? I guess . . . if we're good enough."

"Oh, we're good enough."

Jules shot me a look and went back to her own thoughts, but now she was thinking about our dance company's June 25th Showcase as well as Jack. I smiled to myself. Whatever happened in Jules's life, she'd always be a dancer first. An amazing dancer. If only Linda would give us the new choreography . . .

"Oh, shit!" I exclaimed.

"What? What is it? What happened?"

"Do you know what time it is?"

"Yeah, it's — oh, boy . . . it's almost three o'clock!"

"You do remember we have early rehearsal tomorrow?"

"And we were late to the last one."

"Linda's gonna kill us."

"No, no . . . *kill* is too nice. She's gonna make us dance with Leia."

And, giggling — though it wouldn't seem funny in the morning — we ran for our shoes. On the drive back over the mountain, we talked nonstop, about everything, and nothing. Jack's name never came up. I knew my One and Only. She needed time to work things out in her mind.

Our company, the Fifth Street Dancers, rehearses three times a week at The Belrose, a studio in San Rafael. Linda Marcelle, the director and choreographer, was a student there, then danced professionally in New York until she got married and came back here to teach. She auditioned kids from all over for the company and expected the fifteen she chose to work hard. Which we did, especially right before a show. Jules and I had been with her since the beginning of high school, and our senior year was going to be the best yet. Linda had a tour planned, to Los Angeles, and all the company had to do was raise the money.

For Jules and me, it was perfect timing. We'd dance through the summer and be lean and fit for our senior year, ending high school — and our first nine years of dancing together — with a performance tour in L.A. There'd be one final fund-raiser three weeks before the tour, and if Linda got permission to use the Marin County Performing Arts Center for it, we could be dancing for an audience of almost fourteen hundred people.

It was nine-fifteen when Jules and I arrived at the studio. We hadn't gotten back to my house until almost four in the morning. We'd talked until after five, and two hours later, when the alarm sounded, one of us turned it off. We only woke up because my neighbor's dog was barking to be let in — at ten minutes to nine. We didn't eat, go to the bathroom, brush our teeth, anything. We practically got dressed in the car on the way to the studio.

Linda didn't say a word when we walked in. She simply glanced at us and took a good long look at her watch before she continued leading the class. We knew better than to offer any excuses (Linda: "There are no excuses, only missed opportunities."), so we took our places in the back of the line.

"People who come in late should at least have the sense to warm up a bit before going into stretches," Linda announced to no one in particular. "Even if their company is not important to them, the safety of their bodies should be."

Jules and I went to the barre to do a plié sequence as the rest of the dancers concentrated tremendously on this warmup they knew by heart. Even Brooke didn't dare look at us. If we were lucky, Linda would wind down about halfway through the rehearsal and then we could apologize, *if* we worked hard for the entire time. In the middle of a *tendue* sequence, I snuck a glance to see how Jules was holding up.

She seemed strangely distant, and her technique was very sloppy. Either she was more tired than I realized or Jack was on her mind, because she always put five hundred percent effort into her dancing. Then I remembered the stress, or virus, or whatever she'd been having, and wondered if it had been such a good idea to sit outside in the ocean air all that time. She looked up, and with my eyes, I asked if she was all right. She nodded a tiny nod, and we went on working.

But whatever was bothering her didn't seem to get any better as the rehearsal proceeded. Linda is a perfectionist, so when we were working on the piece with Jules, me, Sarah, and Colleen, she made us do the adagio — the slow part — over and over and over again. It was a seriously difficult combination, all control and strength, and we didn't seem able to get it right, at least not right enough for Linda.

"Nope. Again," she insisted.

She was like a broken record. After almost fifteen takes, she shook her head with frustration, turned, and walked away from us. Sarah and Colleen gave us dirty looks. They had managed their part, and it was because of us we were doing it again and again. I promised God that if I got through this rehearsal, I would never again party the night before Company. I looked to see if Jules was handling it.

She was pale and almost green. Standing with her head bent down and her eyes on the floor, focused on nothing, she was breathing in small gasps, as if she couldn't get her breath.

"Jules?" I put my hand on her shoulder. She didn't answer.

"No talking in rehearsal, please," Linda shot out.

"But Linda, something's wrong with Jules!"

Linda turned back around. Her frustration immediately disappeared, and her mother-self took over.

"Uh-oh. Julie . . . come here, sit down. That's it . . . be careful. Sammie, help me. Easy now."

We brought Jules to the piano bench by the mirror and helped her to sit down. Jules cried out in pain, and tears started down her face. She was breathing sort of raggedy, and her face was cool but sweating. I was getting really scared.

"Are you dizzy?" Linda asked, and then, to Sarah, "Go get me cold towels from the bathroom. Wet and cold."

Jules shook her head and spoke, one word at a time. "Not . . . dizzy . . . just . . . so . . . much . . . OH! . . . pain. It's in my . . . hip . . . and my . . . back. Oh, God, it hurts."

"Should I call her mom?" I asked Linda, who nodded.

She was acting calm, but I could tell she didn't know what to do either. I knew she was afraid somehow she was responsible. I thought doing the same step over and over had probably done it, until I remembered Jules had been having trouble from the very start. I kissed her on the top of her head and went to call Sandra.

Julie

Too embarrassing. Not only had we gotten to the studio late, but I'd messed up the choreography and disrupted the entire rehearsal. I'd cried in front of the whole company because of the stupid pain in my back and my hip. Everyone was mad at me. Linda had barely spoken a word. Then my mother had to come and pick me up.

My hip and back had been aching for the past several weeks, but I hadn't worried that much because they'd both given me trouble before. We were, after all, working full out on the June 25th Showcase, and if you dance, you expect to hurt. Right before we went to rehearsal, the pain had been pretty bad, probably from sitting on the damp sand and not getting enough sleep, and it had gotten steadily worse. When we had to do the adagio, I knew I couldn't hold my leg up in attitude or manage to balance the slow turn. But by then the pain had turned everything sort of hazy and I couldn't say for sure.

I think Sam went with me and my mom, and I think we went to Marin General Hospital's Emergency Room. We belong to Campton Medical, but they're in San Francisco, so we went to the closest place. The admitting nurse was rather nonchalant about what was happening to me, and we had to wait until several bleeding emergencies were handled first. The doctor we finally got took X rays, found nothing broken, and decided it was probably a torn ligament. He gave me some pain pills and told my mom to make sure I stayed off my feet until we saw our own physician. The pills were great. I mean, I have never hurt like I did that Saturday, and they made the pain go away fast. They kinda made me go away, too, if I remember right, but that was okay. I knew Sam and my mom would take care of me.

Waking up later that day, in my own bed with only a little nagging ache in my hip, was incredibly good. I stretched slowly, trying out the parts, afraid of a repeat of the morning. When I had finished the entire inventory and only had a bit more than the usual soreness Linda gives out at each rehearsal, I smiled. For a minute. Then Brooke's party smashed down at me.

Looking over at the phone, I thought about calling Jack and telling him exactly what I felt about his new girlfriend and his wanting "to be the one to tell me." Instead, I called Sam. Her phone rang almost ten times before she answered.

"Hmmm? Whozit?"

"What are you doing sleeping?" I looked over at my clock. "It's four in the afternoon!"

"Jules, is that you, my own true friend, come back from the dead?"

"Don't be funny — that hurt!"

"You shoulda seen how you looked — you woulda really been in pain."

"Thank you, my best friend."

"Serious. Are you okay? You scared me. A lot."

"You shoulda been on this side of it."

"Was it from dance?"

"I don't know. I don't think so. Maybe stress or something, or maybe sitting out at Stinson. It didn't get real bad until that combination."

"Don't even mention that combination!"

"Is Linda really mad?"

"Linda loves your funky ass. Plus I think she thinks she's the one who hurt you. She was scared."

"Right. And Jack's new girlfriend looks like Michelle Pfeiffer."

"Are you still thinking about that creep?"

"No, actually, I'm completely over him. Of course I'm thinking about him. I love him. And I want to hurt him now. A lot."

"Yeah?"

"Yeah. You got any ideas?"

"As a matter of fact, now that you ask . . ."

"Yeah?"

"You don't have to do anything. Just wait."

"For what?"

"The June 25th Showcase."

"Sam, you're not making any sense."

"No? Think about it. Dancing and Jack."

"Yeah?"

"Don't you remember the look on his face when he used to watch you in class?"

"That was when he was in love with me."

"No, dear. That was pure and simple lustful adoration. For you as a dancer. Because you as a dancer are fantastic."

"Right."

"You are. And you know you are. So you just get better and we'll make sure he comes to the show."

"I wish you'd think of something more fun. Like castration by manicure scissors. . . ."

"Mm, tasty. I'll hold him down."

"You sure you have time? It'd take hours. . . ."

"He can't be that big!"

"How would *you* know?"

"This is going to be fun. . . . I can just imagine the look on the Lovely Rachael's face when he can't take his eyes off of you. . . ."

Just then we heard a giggle. It was my little sister, Rosie, on the extension.

"Oh, shit. Is that you, Rosie?" There was silence. "Rosie, I know you're there. Get off or I'll tell Mom. Now." There was another moment of silence. "Rosie!"

"If you tell Mommy, I'll tell Daddy you said 'Oh, shit'!" Rosie answered, and slammed down the phone. I could hear her giggling on the way to her room. Sam laughed, too.

"I wish I had a little sister."

"You wouldn't if you did. Do you think she understood what we were saying?"

"Jules, she's only five."

"Yeah, well, I don't want her repeating it to my mom."

"She won't. Now what about my plan?"

"Well, maybe. I don't know."

"What? You got a better idea?"

"No, but . . ."

"Then shut up and concentrate on healing, okay?"

"Yes, ma'am."

"And get my bed ready — I'm coming over. The boyfriend took Mother Dear up to Tahoe till Thursday."

"Good. Bring a pizza. I'm starving."

Sam

School ended and summer started. Jules and I had decided to enroll in Mr. Lipton's U.S. history class for the summer session because we wanted an easier schedule for our senior year. Which was a good idea, but basically meant we only had one week of vacation between finals and the start of summer classes. We'd planned every minute of it. We were going to spend mornings at the beach, afternoons in rehearsal for the concert, and evenings in San Francisco. Then, in August, with the course requirement out of the way, we were going to talk our parents into letting us spend a weekend in Santa Cruz by ourselves.

Only one problem. The pain in Jules's back wouldn't go away, and Sandra spent three weeks dragging her to every doctor she could find. The good part was she got to miss finals. But we hardly even got a chance to talk until the end of our week off.

"Today's reason is ballet," Jules told me on the phone. "It isn't good for the body, you know, especially when you start so young. I should've taken up swimming."

"A doctor told you this?"

"Uh-huh. The one two days ago said it was a pinched nerve. Oh, and 'perhaps a touch of the flu.' "

"I hate this. We missed our whole vacation! Why couldn't you go see these doctors next week, after summer school starts?"

"Because I couldn't."

"Why not? It's probably just stress."

"I don't think so. Anyway, I don't have a choice. I'm sorry you're pissed."

"I'm not pissed. I just miss you."

"Well, hold on — it gets worse. I'm not allowed to dance until we know what it is — so no Showcase."

"Shut up. What doctor told you that?"

"Dr. MOM. And I probably won't be in history with you either."

"At all?"

"Not for the first two weeks, anyway. After that, maybe. Who knows?"

Somehow the weekend passed and I found myself back at Tam High, facing the first day of history without my One and Only. I got there early and took my favorite spot at the back of the room, expecting to see a lot of familiar faces. Missed again. The class was full, but the only person I really knew was Brooke. She did this weird double take when she looked around and saw me but not Jules. I smiled and shrugged, and she smiled back, then found a seat in the front row. A big grinning jock type sat down in the desk next to mine, looked me over, nodded a few times, and said, "Hey." He reminded me of my mother's boyfriend, and his breath smelled bad. Some summer this was starting out to be.

Then Jack walked in, with Rachael attached. They were so busy nuzzling and giggling that they strolled right past without noticing me. For a second, I was glad Jules wasn't there. Then I got mad, because this was exactly what she needed to see. I watched them, thinking how I'd describe it to her on the phone after class.

There were no seats together, so Rachael scrunched her face up and pouted. Jack finally asked this tall, skinny girl to move, and when she did, they sat down next to each other, still attached. When Mr. Lipton started to explain the requirements of the course, Jack turned to get something out of his backpack and saw me. He blanched and looked around for Jules, obviously puzzled that she wasn't there. I ignored him, keeping my eyes on the teacher. Jack finally turned back around and whispered something to Rachael. A second later, she turned and tried to intimidate me by staring. What a freak she was. I stared right back.

At break, I made a point of going up to talk to Brooke, who was almost directly in front of Rachael and Jack. I planned to say something to them as I passed, but they were up and out the door before I could make a sound. Brooke rolled her eyes and shook her head.

"What's their problem?" she said as we both watched them go.

"Who cares? I'm just glad Jules is through with him."

"Where *is* Julie? I thought she was taking this class."

"She has to get her leg fixed. From dance, remember? She'll probably be back next week or the week after."

"It's weird seeing you here by yourself."

"Tell me about it."

Jack and Rachael came back just after Mr. Lipton had started to lecture again, giggling as they did and interrupting the class. Mr. Lipton glared at them.

"Perhaps there's something amusing you'd like to share with the rest of us?"

Rachael turned stone-faced, and Jack shook his head. Mr. Lipton looked from one to the other.

"I see. Good. Well, then, after you've separated yourselves, if indeed that's possible, we will continue the lesson."

He waited until the same tall, skinny girl moved back to her original seat and Jack took her place on the other side of the room. Both Rachael and Jack stared straight ahead with completely blank faces until Mr. Lipton was well into lecturing. When they glanced over at each other, they almost started giggling again. That's when I noticed how bloodshot their eyes were. I sniffed the air in Jack's direction and smiled to myself. Definitely pot. Wait until Jules heard this one.

After class, I grabbed a quick lunch and went to Company rehearsal. I didn't get home until almost four. My mom's car was in the driveway with Bruce's Jag right behind it, so I parked my Jeep on the street and went into the house. They were in the kitchen, laughing so much I was surprised my mom heard me as I tried to make it to my room unnoticed.

"Sammie?" she called out in her Mother Dear voice.

"Yeah, Mom?"

"Honey, guess what? Bruce is cooking dinner for us."

"That's great."

"Yes, I'm a veritable giant in the kitchen," Bruce added, sending my mom into another peal of laughter.

"Whatever," I said, mostly to myself.

I went into my room and shut the door, turned on my radio and dialed Jules. Her line was busy. I tried five more times in the next half hour and gave up when my mom called me in for dinner. It was some kind of baked chicken and rice with sauce and actually smelled quite good. Bruce stood around gloating as my mom served it up.

"This is what you need in a man," she informed me as she handed me a plate, "good looks, a great personality — and he cooks!"

Bruce beamed. "Well, there's absolutely no rule that says a woman has to do all the cooking. And I for one like it that way." He looked meaningfully at me. With my mouth full of chicken, I smiled back.

Then they blew kisses at each other. It caught me by surprise, and the gulp of milk I'd just taken came up through my nose as I started laughing. My mother killed me with her eyes but pretended, for Bruce's sake, to be really concerned.

"Honey . . . Sammie . . . are you all right?" she asked as she patted me on the back and handed me her napkin. I nodded and managed to get myself under control.

"Sorry. It went down the wrong pipe," I explained to Bruce. We continued to eat, in silence but with lots of stupid smiles. Thankfully the phone rang. Assuming it was Jules, I jumped up, but my mom was quicker.

"Hello?" she sang into the receiver. Then her voice changed, and I knew who it was. "Yes, she is. Just a minute." She made a face. "It's for you. Your father."

"I'll take it in my room, okay?"

"Are you through eating?" Behind Bruce's back, she glanced toward him.

"Oh, yeah. Thanks, Bruce. That was really good."

He smiled and nodded, and my mom put the phone on hold. I picked it up on my extension.

"Daddy?"

"Hi, honey, how are you?"

"I'm okay. Did you get my message?"

"I did, I did. As a matter of fact, that's why I'm calling."

I crossed my fingers and held my breath.

"I'm afraid I won't be able to make the recital, Sammie. Ruthie has something planned for us that weekend."

"That's okay. No big deal."

"If it was any other time, you know . . . but this has been in the works now for months . . . well, and she is my wife. . . ."

"It's okay, Daddy. Really."

"Well, there'll be other recitals, now, won't there? No need to feel bad about missing this one."

"Right."

"Well. That's my girl. I knew you'd be mature about it. And, listen, when do I get to see you? I miss you."

"Me, too."

"Well, we'll just have to set up some time. Maybe early next month? Maybe you can come here for a weekend."

"Sure. That'd be good."

"Well, honey, I have to go. It was great talking to you. I love you."

"I love you, too. Thanks for calling."

I sat on my bed, staring at the wall, for almost fifteen minutes, then pulled out my history book and started to read. Somewhere around the Declaration of Independence, I gave up and tried Jules's number again. Sandra answered.

"I'm sorry, Sammie," she told me. "I gave her one of the

pain pills, and she's gone to bed. But she said to tell you she loves you."

"I wish she was going to be in the Showcase." I could feel the whiny note in my voice but couldn't seem to stop it.

Sandra didn't seem to notice.

"I know, sweetie. Me, too. But don't worry. I'm sure she'll dance in the next one. And we'll both be in the audience, you know. To see you."

For some stupid reason, this made me cry.

Julie

The week after the Showcase, we saw Doctor Number 13. I thought maybe because of his number, he'd be the one to figure out what the hell was happening to my body. Oh boy, was I wrong. He fooled us, though, up to the very last. He even looked the part of the kindly Old Family Doctor. He had white hair that frizzed out at one side, and little blue eyes that got crinkly when he smiled. Which he did, a lot. He asked me questions. He asked my mom questions. He read over the history his nurse had taken (we should have had it Xeroxed by now, we'd given out the same information so many times). He looked at the X rays we had sent over from Doctor Number 12. (My mom had decided that enough was enough, we had X rays for ten people and why not just pass 'em along.) He had me lie on my stomach, and he prodded around my back. He had me lie on my back and rotated my hip. He asked me if I'd ever eaten sushi or anything else that might carry parasites (which can attack your joints, I found out later). Then he smiled his warm and friendly Old Family Doctor smile and asked us to come and sit with him in his office.

From behind this huge dark desk, covered with files and an X ray or two (I wondered how he kept them all straight, there were so many), he smiled first at my mother, then at me. Then at my mother once again. When he spoke, his voice was low and mellow, nice to listen to. He looked first at my mom.

"Mrs. Michaels."

His gaze shifted deliberately to me.

"Juliana."

Back to my mom.

"There is no apparent structural or neurological damage. Juliana has full rotation of her hip and more than normal movement in her lower back. The X rays show a slight trauma and therefore possible damage around the ileum, the hip joint, but one could reasonably assume this was the result of her dance career. Quite frankly, although I sympathize with the pain Juliana says she is feeling, I can find nothing wrong."

He paused and looked meaningfully at both of us.

"Except. Well, it isn't my field, but I might suggest you talk to a psychotherapist. It isn't unusual at this age for a girl to have imagined aches and pains. It's a changing time for her, and if there is an area of stress that isn't being properly ventilated, well . . ."

My mother froze. Got really still and focused, like she does when she's about to lay into me for something bad. I knew she was getting ready to make her point, and I knew that when she spoke, her voice would be low and quiet and deadly. I prepared myself. Doctor Number 13 didn't have a clue.

"Well. That's about all I can tell you. Any questions?" he asked.

"Yes." My mother began with an open, easy look on her face. It's how she fools you into thinking she's not really mad. "I understand you to say that my daughter is making this whole thing up. Is that what you mean?"

"Well. 'Making it up' is not exactly what I said. I have no doubt that there is some kind of pain. . . ."

"But you think she's exaggerating it?"

"Ah, yes, possibly. It isn't unusual, as I said."

"You've said absolutely nothing, Doctor. And as far as exaggerating, Julie is a dancer, and dancers quite clearly understand pain. Julie, in fact, has quite a high pain threshold — I've seen it myself the countless times she's been injured. She does not complain. She does not exaggerate. If she tells you the pain is excruciating, it would probably put you or me under the table."

"Mrs. Michaels, now . . . all I can do is offer an educated opinion. I'm not God, you know."

Poor Doctor 13.

"Doctor, I'm under no illusions regarding your place in the universe. Now, let me be quite clear about mine. I've had it with you and all the other doctors here. I'm sick and tired of my daughter having to go through exam after exam, being poked and prodded, X-rayed, tested and retested. And for what?! All we've gotten from you and your colleagues is a runaround." She took a breath and continued.

"Now . . . there is obviously something wrong. I don't know what it is, and Juliana doesn't know what it is. Because we are not doctors. You and the great majority of others in this rather large institution ARE. At least that's what it says on your wall. Therefore, we are simply going to stay. Here. In your office. Until you refer us to someone who will not resort to psychosomatic bullshit because he is unable to make a diagnosis." She glared at him and sat back calmly.

"Now, do you think your nurse would bring us a couple glasses of water while we wait?"

"Mrs. Michaels, let's be reasonable. You can't stay here."

My mom smiled. Her eyes flashed black, and you could hardly hear her, her voice was so low. "No?"

"Absolutely not."

"Move me."

I settled back, smiling to myself. Every bit as much as I hated it when my mom did this number on me, I loved seeing her put the doctor where he belonged. He fumbled a bit as he picked up the phone, then watched us as he waited for someone to answer. It took a few seconds.

"Security, please," he barked, then hung up the phone, sat back, and folded his arms.

I suppose he imagined this would frighten us, but he had sorely underestimated Sandra. When she was my age, she'd been thrown in jail by the San Francisco police for protesting against the Vietnam War. Twice. She wasn't about to be scared by this fool.

Security came, a big beefed-out white guy and a big beefed-out black guy. They must've thought there was a drug addict loose or a guy with a gun or something, because when the doctor indicated us, with one pissy sweep of his arm, they gave him such a look that it was hard not to laugh.

Security White said, "Look, man, I'm not picking up any kid and her mother."

Security Black agreed. "You better call Community Relations, Doc. This isn't our thing."

Community Relations arrived a few minutes later, a rather small man in a nondescript suit and an even smaller woman in a very flowered dress. They smiled and patted me and nodded reassuringly so many times I wondered if their heads were really attached to their shoulders. They looked like those little kissy dolls my grandpa used to have in the back of his big Impala. Doctor 13 was blustery and righteous, but my mom was immovable. I could hardly wait to tell it all to Sam.

Two hours later, she came over, and I did just that. We sat eating tortilla chips in my room. I could feel the pain kinda teasing, but I still had some of the pills, so I didn't worry too much. Even if we didn't know what it was, I could stop it from getting horrible. Sam was on the floor, and I lounged back on my bed.

"So Community Relations won or lost?" she asked.

"Against Sandra? Are you kidding? We have an appointment with Mr. Big-Time Specialist next Wednesday. We also have the flowered lady's 'personal assurance' that 'there will be no holds barred' until we 'ascertain the correct nature of the problem.' "

Sam crunched away. "Is that you, 'the problem'?"

"It's whatever this is. Did you see Jack in class today?"

"Yep," she said with her mouth full. "High again. It's getting to be his normal thing."

"Damn. I wonder why."

"I wonder why you care."

"Do you think it's Rachael?"

"I think I want to talk about something else. How'd you like me in the Showcase?"

"You were amazing."

"Really?"

"Truly." I took a new chip and nibbled the corner, considering a minute. "You know, after his dad died and everything, he was getting high a lot then, too."

"I thought we were talking about me."

"Maybe it's just his escape thing. Like dance is for us."

"I don't think you understand how little I care."

"Actually, I did it once."

"What? You got high with him?"

"Yeah. After his dad's funeral. Down at Old Mill Park."

"Juliana Elise Michaels. You never told me."

"Because I knew you'd be mad."

"I am mad."

"See?"

"I'm not kidding. That sucks."

"Sam — it was months ago."

"I don't care. You're either friends with someone or you're not. And friends don't lie."

We both got quiet. Sam put her chips back in the bag and wiped off her mouth. I lay back against the wall. We didn't look at each other. It was almost five minutes before I spoke.

"I'm sorry."

"Me, too," she answered, and gave me the dirtiest look. "But you're an asshole. Friends don't have secrets."

"Okay. Gotcha."

"I'm serious."

"I know. Am I still your One and Only?"

"Maybe. I'll have to think about it."

"Come on, please?"

"Yeah, you are. But if you *ever* . . ."

"I won't. Promise."

"*Promise* promise?"

"Yes. But you have to go now."

"Why?"

"I'm gonna take a pill, and you know how I get."

"Okay. But first, wait . . . are we gonna go see fireworks this weekend?"

"I don't know."

"How 'bout I'll just come over?"

"That'd be good."

She looked at me carefully. "Are you hurting bad?"

"Not yet. But it's working up to it."

"Jules, I don't like this. I don't like it at all."

"Tell me about it."

She came and sat by me on the bed. I leaned against her. "I wish I could make it go away," she said, "whatever it is."

"Me, too."

"It must be awful to hurt all the time."

"What's really hard is how my mom's started acting. I mean, it was cool how she got in charge at the doctor's office. But she wouldn't have done that if she wasn't scared. And my dad, I don't know what his problem is."

"What's he doing?"

"Just being strange. Not dad-like. You know, dads always know what's going on."

"Trust me. Some dads don't have a clue."

"Yeah, well, mine usually does. But not now. I wish we could find somebody to figure out what's going on and then fix it."

"Maybe this guy next Wednesday."

"I hope."

Sam

Wednesday, the day Jules and Sandra had their appointment with the Big-Time Specialist, I went to class but couldn't concentrate on anything but Rachael and Jack. I sat two rows behind them in class, stared at the back of their heads, and schemed. I wanted to cause them trouble and make them feel stupid. I passed a note to Brooke detailing Part One of my plans. She read it and gave me a thumbs-up.

At break, they disappeared as usual, but we found them sitting in his car, wrapped around each other and lost to the world. I knocked on the passenger window, and Rachael reluctantly rolled it down. Ignoring her (and the smoke drifting out of the car), I leaned over and spoke directly to Jack.

"Julie just wanted me to say thank you." I smiled and raised my eyebrows.

"For what?" he asked. Brooke and I exchanged knowing glances.

"*You* know what," Brooke said, leaning down over my shoulder with an evil smile. Rachael didn't say a word, just got even uglier as she imagined what she thought we meant. Of course, Jack immediately got defensive.

"Leave me alone, would you? I haven't even seen Juliana."

"Oh, right," I said, smiling. "Must have been some other tall, blond boy, huh, Brooke?"

"Must've been." We laughed as we walked away, and Rachael started to whine almost immediately.

Now, if somebody did that to *my* boy, I would know in a minute if he was fooling around or if he really didn't know what she was talking about. I learned that from my mom, when she used to confront my dad about not coming home. It's easy. If you watch the eyes, you can always tell if they're lying. So instead of looking at us, Rachael should have been watching Jack. She would've seen that he didn't have Clue One what we were saying. But by the time she got around to checking him out, he looked guilty as hell because he was trying so hard not to.

Brooke and I laughed all the way back to the history classroom.

"Betcha they won't be back to class today," she said.

"Well, it serves them right. Okay, are you ready to help with Part Two?" I told her the best part of my scheme.

"I don't know, Sammie. That's pretty low."

"Come on, you can't back out now."

"I don't think it's such a great idea."

"Fine. I'll do it myself."

"Don't be mad."

"I'm not."

"Yes, you are."

"I just don't understand what the big deal is. We're not lying or anything."

"I know, but . . ."

"Look, whatever. I just thought you and Jules were

better friends. This is really for her, you know."

"I know. But, anyway, break's almost over. Mr. Lipton gets mad if we're late."

"We could get a note."

She looked over and rolled her eyes up, and I knew I had her. We dropped our books on a desk and hurried to see Mr. Watson, the dean of students.

He was kicked back in his office, as usual, with most of the girls soccer team hanging out with him. We stopped in the doorway, acting like we weren't sure we wanted to be there, like maybe we had something to say that made us nervous. He picked up on it right away and asked the girls to take a hike. Brooke and I snuck a look at each other. Maybe we shoulda been actors instead of dancers.

He closed the door. We sat down on his little office couch and kept looking at each other and our shoes. He waited. I sighed, glanced up, and looked down again.

"Okay, Brooke, whatcha got?" (Good old Mr. Watson — right to the point.)

"I don't know if I should tell you."

"All right. Samantha?"

"Well, we're worried."

"Yes?"

"But we don't want to get anyone in trouble."

"Girls," he said, knowing he must say this very thing two million times a year, "you can't *get* anyone in trouble. People get themselves in trouble. If you want me to know this, whatever it is, just say it. If you don't, I was in the middle of a conversation."

"Right," I answered him. "Okay. We're worried about Jack and Rachael."

He waited quietly.

"We think they're coming to class high," I said. "Or if they're not, they're acting like they are."

"It's funny," he said, looking slowly from me to Brooke. "I didn't think you liked Jack anymore. Since he's not with Julie, I mean. So why would you be so concerned?"

There was a long stretch of silence, and my stomach turned over. Brooke shot me a nervous glance before answering, "You don't have to like someone to worry what happens to them, you know."

"That's true," he said.

"Besides," I added, opting for partial truth, "Julie still likes him. And we wouldn't want to see him do something he might be sorry for later on."

Mr. Watson shifted his eyes from me to Brooke and back to me. We both kept our faces composed and concerned. He shrugged before speaking.

"Okay, girls. I'll look into it. I suppose you need a note?"

Brooke punched me in the arm as soon as we got out the door, but waited until we were out of the building to speak.

"Thanks a lot."

"What? Nothing happened."

"Yeah? See if I ever listen to you again."

"Chill, okay? It's fine. You were great." I started laughing. "Especially when he brought up Jules. You should've seen your face."

"Yeah, well, I still think it's a low blow. Even if it is Jack and Rachael. And Julie's not going to like it, either. You wait and see."

"You don't know her like I do."

I looked at my watch as we went back into class. Jules should almost be home from the doctor's by now. I sat down next to the window as Brooke gave Mr. Lipton the note. He took it and nodded, then continued with his lecture.

Outside, I could see Mr. Watson striding across the parking lot, right up to Jack's car. He leaned down on the driver's side and a second later, both Jack and Rachael were getting out. They did not seem happy as they walked with him back toward his office. Rachael glanced toward the classroom, and I leaned away from the window and smiled to myself. I tried to catch Brooke's eye, but she was either too busy taking notes or just wanted to ignore the whole thing.

The instant class ended, I rushed to the phone to call Jules. The line was busy. I waited a minute and tried again but got the same. It was frustrating. I thought about going over there, but as much as I wanted to know what was happening and tell her what we'd done, I really didn't want to barge in on anything. I'd go home and wait for her to call. Just then, Mr. Watson walked out with Jack and Rachael and some woman I assumed was Rachael's mom. She wasn't happy. I ducked behind the phone booth until they finished talking and Mr. Watson went back inside. Rachael and her mom walked off toward the visitors' parking lot. I was so into watching them, I didn't see Jack approach.

"I thought that was you," he said, not a bit giggly.

"Damn! You scared me."

"Do you have a minute to talk?"

"Not really, why?"

"Because that was a shitty thing you did today."

"It was a joke. We were just giving you a bad time."

"I mean telling Mr. Watson."

"Telling him what? I didn't even talk to him today."

"Okay, fine, I don't care. Just please stay away from me, all right? Your shit is getting boring."

"Oh, really."

"Yeah. I never did anything to you, and my relationship with Julie is none of your business."

"Oh? What relationship is that? The one where you use her or the one where you dump on her?"

He didn't answer, just snorted and shook his head and walked away. Too bad. I didn't feel the least bit uncomfortable about getting him in trouble. He deserved it. I got in my car. There was no rehearsal scheduled, so I started for home. Until I remembered my mom was there. She was too weird these days — half the time yelling at me and the other half floating around the house being in love. Maybe it was early menopause. I decided to go to the library and get all my history homework out of the way. Just in case something . . . well, just in case Jules needed me to drop by later.

Julie

Tuesday night hadn't been so good for me. I'd taken a pain pill, but it was almost like the pain had gotten used to them, and nothing happened. My mom said I couldn't take another for at least three more hours, so I just lay there. I tried to focus my mind off of my body. It didn't work. The pain had taken over. It trapped me in myself. I couldn't talk to my mom, not really. I couldn't watch TV or listen to the radio. I just kept coming back to this alien monster that had taken up residence in my body. It was eating me up. I couldn't see around it or through it, and I couldn't make myself believe it would ever go away.

Two and a half hours went by. At least that's what the clock said. I couldn't have told you because time didn't have any kind of significance anymore. My mom called a friend who is a doctor (she was past trusting the doctors we'd already seen) and found out the pain medication could be doubled safely and that it wouldn't hurt me to have the dosage now. I was vaguely aware of her lifting my head and getting me to open my mouth and swallow the pills, but that's all. Then . . . finally . . . I could breathe again. I could see, and I could be in the world. The double dosage worked its magic, and I started to come around. Sleep hit almost immediately.

The pills wore off in the early morning, but for some reason the monster didn't return as strong as he'd been the night before. It was about five A.M., and I could hear my mom, who hates to get out of bed before seven, in the kitchen making coffee. I went out to join her.

"Hey, Mom," I said as I sat down slowly at the table.

"Hi, sweetie. How're you feeling?"

"Not great, but not as bad as last night."

"Good." She poured her coffee into the grotesque green and orangey mug I'd made for her in ceramics in ninth grade. I don't know why she uses it so much, but she does. It's her favorite cup.

"Want some breakfast?" she asked, setting the cup on the table by her chair.

"I don't think so. Maybe juice."

She poured a glass of orange juice, served me, and sat down. She looked worn out. I had the thought that it must be hard getting old. My mom was gonna turn forty-two this year and was beginning to show her age. When she looked down, as she was now to sip at the hot coffee, the lines in her face were deep. I reached my hand out and petted her cheek, like she used to do to me when I was a little kid.

"You look tired," I told her.

"A little, I guess."

"Are you worried?" I asked, not sure at all that I wanted an answer. My mom took a deep breath, then let it out before answering.

"Yeah, I am. Are you?"

I nodded and sipped my orange juice, then asked, "What are we gonna do if it's something really bad?"

My mom looked straight in my eyes. She reached over and took my hand in hers.

"If it *is* something bad, which it probably won't be, we will take care of it, together. Okay?"

"Okay."

"I love you."

"I know. I love you, too."

"I love you three!" said a little voice, and my sister, Rosie, poked her head around the corner. I grimaced — she always seemed to pick the wrong times to intrude, but I guess that's what five-year-olds do. Mom patted her lap, and Rosie climbed up.

The appointment was at nine that morning. After dropping Rosie at Sunburst Preschool, in Mill Valley, we went over the Golden Gate Bridge to Campton Medical Center, in San Francisco. We sat in the waiting room by the designated office, down a hall painted with lines of different colors. We had followed the pink line and ended up there, all alone.

Apparently my Big-Time Specialist was coming to the hospital that day just for us. I couldn't wait to see what he looked like and was surprised when he was a she. Her name was Dr. Angela Conner. She was large, but not fat, with a squarish body, thick legs, and arms that looked equipped to handle any emergency. Her brown-gray hair was pulled back in a ballet bun, and I couldn't help thinking how ridiculous she'd look at the barre. She had an air about her that made me believe she knew what she was doing and would waste no time doing it. She had opened the door herself — no nurses here — and was giving me the once-over. I don't even think she saw my mom.

"Juliana Michaels?" she asked in a no-nonsense kind of voice.

I nodded.

"Come," she said, gesturing with her head to the inside office. Then she walked back through the door.

I looked at my mom, and she shrugged. We got up, opened the door, and saw Dr. Conner disappearing into an examining room. We came to the door, and she spoke to my mom.

"You wait there, please," she said, indicating the hall.

"No. I'm coming in," my mom replied, using *her* no-nonsense voice.

Dr. Conner took a first good look at her and nodded. We all went in. I waited to be asked all the same questions, then noticed my chart was already there. I started to get undressed, so she could examine me, but she shook her head.

"No need to do what's already been done. Your information shows many possibilities have already been eliminated. You are still hurting?"

I nodded. "That's for sure."

"Has it become worse than before?"

"Mmm-hmm."

"How much worse?"

"I don't know. It's pretty bad."

She looked down for a minute, then back to me before she spoke. "I would like to suggest a bone marrow examination."

"What is that?" I asked.

"Not a pleasant test. It hurts, but probably not as bad

as what you're going through now. A needle is put in here." She indicated a place by my hip. "We take a sample of the marrow inside the hip. There is a one-night stay in the hospital, so that we can medicate well for pain afterward."

"What does it do? This test?" I asked.

"I won't authorize any more useless testing," my mom interrupted. "You must be absolutely sure it's necessary."

"I understand. Julie has been through a lot without much return. We do know there is no apparent nerve damage, no injuries, no obvious viral infection — but we cannot be sure of more until we take the sample. I will do the procedure myself. I am good at what I do, and I will try not to hurt her too much. I feel it is the only reasonable next step. If you agree."

"But what does it do? What does it test *for?*" I asked again. My mom jumped in before the doctor had a chance to speak.

"It lets us know exactly what all this is about, sweetie. So we don't have to keep seeing different doctors. And we can get you well and dancing again."

"That is basically correct," Dr. Conner added, nodding at my mom.

I looked at them both. I was relieved somebody was finally believing me, and I liked the way this woman talked. I shrugged and nodded. My mom nodded, too.

"Yes. We agree," she said. "When should we have it done?"

"Soon. Today if possible. You could check in now, and I would do the procedure late this afternoon. Did you eat breakfast?"

"Only juice."

"That's good. Is that all right, today?"

"Well, uh . . . okay, I suppose so," my mom said. "I'd like to call my husband first, though."

"Come with me. I'll show you a phone. Juliana can stay here and rest."

They walked out of the examining room, and I hoisted myself up on the table. I was dizzy all of a sudden. Everything was moving so fast these days. The night Sam and I spent on the beach seemed like only a few days ago, but it had been just over a month. A month of not being able to go to dance except for a few days, a month of horrible pain, a month of not even seeing Jack — not that he cared. Thank God for Sam, I thought. She'd been over or called almost every day. She'd brought me stories and kept me up on what was happening at dance and at summer school. Now, finally, I was going to be able to find out what this was all about and hopefully get it fixed and get back to normal. It was a lousy way to spend my summer. I lay back on the table and closed my eyes. There was too much to think about, and I was tired. But for the first time in weeks, I started to imagine myself without all this pain.

I must've fallen asleep, because the next thing I remember was my mom stroking my face and saying softly, "Julie . . . Julie, honey. Time to wake up. Come on, sweetie, we have to go downstairs."

I opened my eyes and closed them again. "Where are we going?" I asked her.

"I've got you checked in to your room. For the test, remember? Dr. Conner is going to do your bone marrow test."

I groaned. All I could think of now was the pain. It had

been relatively easy that morning, and I didn't feel like having more.

"Do I really have to?"

"Sweetie, I don't know what else to do. She's the only doctor you've seen that sounds like she knows what she's talking about. Maybe we ought to listen — you think?"

"I just want it to be over, Mommy."

"Me, too, baby — me, too."

Sam

I finished all my homework about four and stopped at The Depot to call Jules. No answer. I had some fruit salad and then tried again. Still no answer. I decided to go over. There was only one car in the driveway when I got there, and it wasn't the one Sandra usually drove. I parked my Jeep and went to the front door and knocked. No one came. I walked around the side.

"Hello? It's Sammie. Anybody here?"

"Hello, Sammie." I jumped back, startled. It was William, Jules's dad, coming around the corner from the back.

"Shit, you scared me. Oh, sorry," I said, remembering he didn't like us to swear. Then I realized he hadn't even noticed.

"They're not back yet. Julie has to have some other kind of test."

"Oh. So they didn't find out anything?"

He shook his head. "Would you like something to drink? Juice? Soda?" he asked. "Oh, and there's some cookies Sandra made."

William is known for being the politest of all the fathers in our group of friends. I shook my head.

"No, thanks. I'm not hungry."

"Julie has to stay at the hospital, for the test. I'm going in to visit her later."

"Oh." I tried not to sound as disappointed as I felt. "So she won't be home at all?"

"Not tonight. Say, would you like to come with me?"

"I sure would. What time?"

He didn't answer right away.

"Uh, maybe I should go in my own car . . . ," I offered.

"Oh, no, it's all right. It's fine. You can drive with me. Sandra's going to stay straight through. We'll leave around six-thirty, after traffic."

"Okay." I waited, shrugged. "I guess I'll see you then?"

"Yes, good. Six-thirty."

He smiled sort of absently and nodded, then turned and started walking back.

"William?" I called. He looked at me. "Are you feeling okay?"

He nodded. "Oh, yes, I'm fine," he said. "Just preoccupied. But she'll be all right soon. She will. She's young and strong."

At seven-oh-three, William and I pulled up to Campton Medical. We hadn't said more than two words the whole way, and the drive had seemed endless. The visitors' parking lot was packed. It took ten minutes to find a space, and then almost twenty-five more to find Jules. It seemed like we walked up and down every corridor in the whole damn place before we saw Sandra standing outside a door. She saw us at the same time and came over, motioning with her finger to be quiet. She gave us both a hug before she spoke.

"She's just waking up," she said. "From what I can gather, it seems to have gone smoothly."

William nodded and smiled.

"What exactly did they do?" I asked.

"They took some bone marrow out to test it."

"Why?"

"Probably because they didn't know what else to do to her," said William sarcastically. Sandra put her arm around his waist and looked at me.

"It's been hard not to worry a lot when the doctors have been so . . . difficult," she said. "But I think we're coming to the end of it now. Julie was a champ."

"Can I go in and see her?" I asked

"Give her a minute. The doctor is still there."

A moment later, Giganta Woman walked over to us, and Sandra introduced Dr. Conner. Obviously not one for wasting words, she nodded at us and addressed herself directly to Sandra.

"The marrow sample is down at Pathology now. I'd like to meet with Julie and the two of you as soon as I get conclusive results. Are you available tomorrow morning, around nine?"

"Doctor, we'll meet you at midnight if we can find out what's wrong with our girl," William told her.

Dr. Conner nodded once. "Nine, then. Here in her room." She nodded again, turned, and walked away.

I looked at William and Sandra and then at Giganta Woman lumbering down the hall. She knew something already, I could tell. Why didn't she say it? And why hadn't Jules's parents asked?

Julie

My mom had left me at the door in Pre-Op, the coldest room ever built, and a nurse covered me with some thin space-age blanket that turned out to be quite warm. The IV needle had been put into my arm, and the anesthesiologist, Dr. Kim, had commented on the healthy size of my veins. Dr. Conner was now explaining "The Procedure" to me, in depth, with her award-winning tact, and if I hadn't been in so much pain, I would've been terrified. But IT had returned, and IT was pissed off, so even though I was looking at the doctor and nodding in what I hoped were suitably appropriate places, I was only getting a general idea of what she was trying to say. I only started really listening when she got to the part about the Valium.

" . . . will not put you under exactly but will take away the pain [HOORAY!!] and the immediacy of the experience. Are you ready?"

I nodded. Just say yes, I thought. Dr. Kim inserted something into the IV tube, and the orderly, or whoever it is that moves beds, got ready to go to the Operating Room. I could get used to this, I remember thinking as I drifted into Twilight World. No pain, no problems. I could hear everything that was going on around me, but

I didn't have to respond to it. Probably I would have been able to see, too, but since it seemed a more pleasant choice to keep my eyes shut, that's what I did.

I felt myself transferred to another bed. I knew Dr. Conner was in the room and giving orders. Someone sat near my head and kept putting a cool, wet towel on my lips, and I would smack them and swallow the moisture. Every once in a while, a voice I didn't recognize but nevertheless liked the sound of asked if I was feeling okay. "Jusss fine," I would answer, then float some more. Time had no meaning, pain did not exist, there was nothing in the world I had to think on, worry about, or do. I thought I had arrived in Paradise.

Three hours later, I wasn't so sure. The Valium had worn off, and whatever the anesthesiologist had slipped in the IV as I was being wheeled back to my room — "Here's a little whammy to help with the pain," he'd said, not asking if I wanted it — was not in agreement with my system. I got horribly nauseated and vomited violently — on the bed, on the nurse, on the floor. Over and over, missing the bedpan each time, until another nurse insisted on calling the doctor. It seemed years before she came.

"Are you hurting?" was the first thing she asked.

"Not yet," I replied, and tried to vomit on her.

"It's nothing to worry about," she assured me. "You're having a reaction to the pain medication. It happens to many people."

Whatever I would've said to respond wouldn't have been appreciated, and I couldn't have got it out between vomits anyway, so I just nodded.

"I'm ordering an anti-nausea medication."

"What if it makes me sick, too?"

"I don't think it will. Trust me."

Right.

By the time my parents and Sam came in, I had entered Phase Three. Over the Procedure, past the drug reactions, and now responding to the sleep inducer. I tried to smile at them, tried to let them know that I was finally feeling better, but nothing I said seemed to make any sense. They kept smiling at me and patting me, and then they left me alone with Sam for a minute. I managed to reach out my hand. She took it. She read my mind, as she usually does, and answered what I was unable to ask.

"They don't know anything yet, Jules. The doctor's meeting with you guys in the morning. Nine o'clock. After she sees what those tests have to say. How 'bout now — are you feeling okay?" I nodded. "Do you need anything?" I shook my head. "Well, then let me tell you what I did today . . ." and she flashed her wicked look. I couldn't keep my eyes open too well, but my ears were working, and as she told me the story of Jack and The Freak and then the part about the dean, I smiled and smiled and smiled.

Next morning, a nurse woke me at five to take my temperature and ask me stupid questions. I managed to go back to sleep, only to be awakened again by a different one. Temperature again, same stupid questions.

"You guys already did this once," I told her. She gave me her Indulgent Nurse Smile.

"I'm the new shift," she explained.

Oh. Fine. The fact that I couldn't get back to sleep didn't seem to concern her. The fact that my hip, where the needle had gone in, was now on fire didn't seem to, either.

"Could I please have something for this pain?" I asked. She gave me her Concerned Caregiver Face.

"I'm sorry," she dripped, "but Dr. Conner didn't indicate any medication on your chart."

"Would you call her, or something, please? This really hurts."

"Well, she'll be in at eight-thirty. Let's ask her then, shall we?"

"Okay." She smiled again and started to leave. "Excuse me," I said, "Could you tell me what time it is now?"

"Seven-fifteen." And she was gone.

An hour and fifteen minutes is not a long time under the best of circumstances. I, however, was not under those kind. I hurt, I was tired and cranky, my mouth tasted like *caca,* and I wanted my mother. Or Sam. Or somebody. Plus I did not want to think about the meeting with Dr. Conner.

Eight-thirty came and went. No doctor, at least according to Miss Happy-Face. A few minutes later, my mom and dad showed up. I was in pretty bad shape. I didn't know which part of me hurt the worst.

The second he saw me, my father was furious.

"This is ridiculous," he announced to no one in particular, and went to get help. My mom stroked my face and talked softly, about nothing, really, just to keep my mind occupied. My dad came back, nurse in tow, with Dr. Conner right behind. No smiles this time. The nurse took a vial and inserted its contents into the IV tube. She'd obviously been spoken to by the doctor. Almost immediately, the pain started to go. I sighed. Nurse Happy left, and Dr. Conner checked my pulse and felt my forehead.

"No excuse for that, I'm afraid," she told us. "The medication was indicated." My dad started to open his mouth, but Dr. Conner wasn't through. "There are chairs right outside. Let's pull a few in here and have a little talk."

A chill like ice cut through my entire body. My mouth went dry. I wondered if maybe I was having another reaction to the medication, but then I looked at my mom. She was a ghost. My dad pulled a couple of chairs in, next to the bed, but both my parents remained standing. Dr. Conner stood across from them and looked at me as she talked.

"As I suspected it might, the marrow shows that you have diffuse histiocytic lymphoma. Because it has shown up in the marrow, we can assume it is Stage Four. This means it did not originate in the hip. The hip is a secondary site, and there are undoubtedly other affected areas. My recommendation is an immediate aggressive program of chemotherapy. Your age is a definite advantage. Your body can withstand much more than an older, adult body can. This increases our chances significantly."

She paused a moment and smiled encouragingly, then continued. "We can do the therapy here, or if you would like, arrange for an outpatient facility. Of course, certain side effects may occur — severe nausea, weight gain or loss, skin disorders, and low blood count, which means you will have to take extra care against infection. Oh, and almost everyone has loss of hair. I would be happy to orchestrate the program, if you so desire, or I can put you in touch with other oncologists. I welcome a second opinion, should you wish to seek one, but I recommend you do it immediately. Time is of utmost importance in cases of this type." She peered at each of us. "I think I've covered everything. Do you have any questions?"

Almost out of breath from listening to her, I realized I had understood only part of what she had been saying. I looked at my parents and saw the same confusion. My mother asked the question.

"Doctor, you need to tell us . . . exactly what is diverse histiowhatever?"

"Diffuse histiocytic lymphoma" — she paused, sighed — "is a type of cancer."

She continued speaking, explaining, but it didn't matter what she said after she said the C-word. We didn't hear any of it. We'd find out later, as we lived it, but just then, we couldn't move. We didn't look at each other. We didn't speak. I don't think we were even breathing. Dr. Conner murmured something about giving us some time, then left the room. My father sat down. My mother stayed frozen by my bed. Except for her hand. It walked across the bed and found my cheek. She stroked me, softly, over and over, like she'd done when I was three and fretful, or thirteen with my first broken heart. Then she made herself move, and she turned to look in my eyes. My father stood up and came to the other side of the bed. He didn't make a sound, but tears were running down his face, and I remember thinking, Hey, this is weird — I've never seen my father cry.

No one said a word. What was there to say? I had cancer.

Sam

Sixty-year-old men who have smoked their whole lives get cancer or women who don't do Pap smears or forget to check their breasts. People in other countries get it, or other states or other towns. But not a sixteen-year-old beautiful dancer girl who has never done anything bad to anyone in her entire life. Not my best friend.

I had ditched school the next morning and gone to San Francisco to Campton Medical. Priorities are priorities. I got up to Jules's room pretty soon after Dr. Conner had left, I guess. I knocked and when no one answered, peeked my head in. Sandra and William were on either side of Jules, and they were all three holding on to each other. Jules was the only one not crying. I knew right then it was something bad — real bad. Part of me wanted to just turn around, right there and then, and go away. Forever. If I didn't hear whatever it was, maybe then it wouldn't actually be. But I didn't move. I stood where I was, waiting.

Jules saw me first. The minute our eyes locked, she started to cry. Soft, no sound, just tears coming down.

"Is it fucked?" I asked.

She nodded.

"Cancer." She whispered it so lightly I almost didn't hear. Then the word flew over and smacked me.

I stopped, as in ceased. Completely, utterly, no life in me for what seemed like years. Immense silence descended. I could only hear my heart. Everything else had moved outside my range of perception. Nothing was possible — not speech, not tears, not thought.

Sandra came over and led me to Jules. I kept staring at her. I shook my head. I kept trying to make my brain start functioning again. I wanted one of them to say, "Ha, ha — just teasing." I wished I could go back to yesterday and skip right to tomorrow, so this could not occur.

Then I wanted to laugh. Bubbles of it came up from inside, and there wasn't a thing I could do to stop them. Sounds started coming out — rigid, ugly sounds — and I wanted to tell Jules I was sorry, I really didn't think it was funny, that I didn't mean to laugh, but I couldn't stop. The sounds kept pouring out. All of a sudden, it wasn't laughing anymore — it was tears. My Jules, my Juliana Dancer Girl, my One and Only, reached out and pulled me in. I put my arms around her and we cried. And cried.

I'm not too clear on the rest of the day. I couldn't tell you when I left the hospital or how I drove back over the bridge to my house. When my mother asked how everything was, I don't know why the words came out sounding normal and easy. I do remember lying, not wanting my mom to know anything about anything, at least not then. She's not the kind of woman who can deal with things. She always overreacts. She would call the Michaelses; she would ask them and me an endless assortment of stupid questions. It would only make me mad.

Besides, this was too important. No one who was on the outside could know. Not yet. It belonged only to me and Jules and her family. So I just said "fine" when she asked how Jules was, and went into my room.

I remember I turned on the radio and then I reorganized my history notes and rewrote all the due dates for my school assignments in a different organizer. I read the same paragraph in my history book four times, and somehow I finished my homework. Then I went out and did the dishes. Around midnight, I started cleaning my room. That was good until an old scrapbook emerged from the bottom of my closet.

Jules and I had put it together in eighth grade, page after page of collages, using pictures and words from magazines, and even cutting out photos from the yearbook. I could remember doing it, right there in my room, giggling and cussing, trying out all our bad language and exercising our newly acquired slang. Our entire middle school experience was summed up; what we thought, who we liked, what we wanted to grow up to be, who we wanted to kill. I laughed until tears came out. When I finished, I sat holding it close to my body. I thought maybe I should be crying, but there didn't seem to be any tears available. Knowing I wouldn't be able to sleep, I tried to figure out something else to do. I couldn't, and my body was too tired anyway. Finally I made myself think about now, and I made myself say it out loud.

"Jules has cancer. My best friend, Jules, has cancer."

Then silence. I could almost see the word hanging in the air around my head. I conjured up whatever I thought I knew about it. It occurred to me then that I didn't really understand what it meant, not specifically in relation to

Jules. Sandra had explained as much as she could, but she didn't really know, either.

Obviously then, the first thing would be to go to the library and read up on it. I would be able to tell how worried I should be or if I needed to be worried at all. Hey, Jules was young, strong, and a fighter. This could be over sooner than we thought. Maybe it was the kind of cancer you could get an operation for. So — it would be a hard few months and then everything would be okay. We could get back to being normal. It didn't matter if we didn't dance or go on tour or do the concert. It didn't matter if stupid Jack stayed with The Freak forever.

The one important thing in the whole world was to have Jules be well. But how could she not be? She was my One and Only. We were together in this world, and nothing could change that, ever.

Julie

One strange thing about Being In A Crisis, especially being at the center of one, is how everything else just keeps moving along. You don't think it will. You don't see how it can. When Dr. Conner stood at the side of my bed and delivered her news, it felt like every other part of the world should have reacted to what had just happened in mine. The nurses should have paused, traffic in the streets should've pulled over, babies should've stopped crying. Just for a minute, just to acknowledge that for some reason, my life had changed. But nobody seemed to notice. Even Dr. Conner. She dropped her bomb, nodded at us, and left. And the day went on.

We crashed, me and my parents and my Sam. Then we went on, too. That's the other strange thing about A Crisis. When you're outside of it, not touched by it, you say, "Oh, my God, how do they stand it? Poor things, how could they live through that?" When it's around you, in you, you simply do it. Because there's no choice. Only a next step.

We got a second opinion of course, that same morning. By the time it came around, we were ready for it. Definitely diagnosed, we decided Dr. Conner, for all of her lack of tact, was probably one of the better doctors Campton Medical had to offer, and we asked her to handle the treatment. She suggested an outpatient facility on our side of the Golden Gate, and we made an appointment to start chemotherapy the following day. All of this happened in less than five more hours. Then we went home.

My dad drove. My mom sat in the backseat with me, and no one talked. I could see my dad's face in the rearview mirror. He was pissed. My mom, on the other hand, never stopped smiling this not-Sandra-like smile and kept brushing nonexistent hairs away from my face. Halfway across the bridge, my dad flipped on the radio, and we finished the ride into Mill Valley listening to Motown from the sixties.

We parked in our driveway, and my dad looked back at my mom. "Do you need help getting her into the house?"

My mom shook her head, still smiling.

"I can walk, Daddy." He didn't seem to hear me, just kept staring at my mom.

"We're fine, William." He nodded and got out. Rosie and her friend Katie came bounding over from across the street, with Katie's mom, Donna, close behind. My mom and I were halfway out of the car when Rosie reached my dad at full speed and jumped. He caught her up in his arms, stumbled a bit, and backed into the open car door. It bumped me, not hard, but directly on the spot where Dr. Conner had drilled. I yelped. Rosie was too excited to notice.

"Can I have a sleepover at Katie's, Daddy? Pleasepleasepleaseplease, oh, Daddy, please. . . ."

He set her down roughly. "How many times have I told you you're getting too big to jump on me like that? You see what you did?" Rosie's face crumbled.

"I'm okay, Daddy — she didn't mean it."

"That's not the point," he said, and turned back to Rosie. "You have to learn to think before you act. Do you understand me?" Rosie nodded, beginning to tear. "You might have really hurt your sister. Now, what do you say?"

"I'm sorry, Daddy," Rosie managed in a tiny voice before she started to cry for real. My mom stood there looking helpless, and Katie backed up next to Donna.

"Why don't I call you later, Sandra," Donna said, and led Katie back across the street. My mom nodded. Rosie slithered down and disappeared into the house. Silent and stiff, my dad followed. My mom looked at me and started smiling that stupid smile again.

"Well, let's get you inside, shall we?"

Things got even stranger when we went inside the house. Rosie was crying in her bedroom. My dad was banging around the kitchen, fixing himself a cup of coffee. My mom just kept smiling.

"How are you feeling, sweetie?" Her voice didn't sound like it belonged to her.

"I'm okay, I guess. Maybe a little hungry."

"Good. How about some soup or something?"

"Mom? What about Rosie?"

"Hmm?"

"She's crying an awful lot."

My mom turned her head and seemed to hear it for the first time.

"You want to go see her?" I asked. "I can fix the soup."

"Maybe that's best." She patted me and went off to comfort my sister.

I'd never seen her like this. My dad, either. He had turned into a zombie. As I stood in the kitchen, opening a can of split pea soup, he sat at the kitchen table, staring straight ahead.

"You want some, Daddy?" I said as I stirred it into the pot.

"No, thanks."

I poured myself a bowl and sat down at the table. He got up and went into the living room. I finished my soup alone. My mom came in with Rosie just as I was washing out my dish. She had stopped crying but was clinging to Mom's leg.

"I'm sorry, Julsie," she whimpered. "I didn't mean to hurt you."

"No big deal, shortie. C'mere and give me a kiss." She did, but tentatively, then sidled over to Mom again.

"How are you feeling, sweetie?" my mom asked, again.

"I'm fine."

"Did you get enough to eat?"

"Yeah."

"How about the pain? Is it, uh, okay? Do you want to take one of the pills Dr. Conner gave you?"

"I don't think so. Not yet."

"All right, well, you let me know if you need anything. I'm going to fix the rest of us something to eat." She sat Rosie down at the kitchen table.

"Great." I smiled at her smiling at me, then went into the living room. My dad was reading the paper.

"How are you, Daddy?" I asked him.

"Just fine, thanks." He didn't look at me. I sat down on the couch. No one was talking, no TV was on, no Rosie-voice was chirping around the house. There was nothing to keep me from hearing Dr. Conner's words over and over in my head. Finally I went in my room and put on some music. I felt like the whole thing was my fault. I had screwed everything up. Maybe if I apologized? I dialed Sam but hung up before it rang. I wasn't ready to talk yet.

I drifted off for a while, until the pain woke me up. It wasn't horrible, but it was definitely there. This would be a good time to use Dr. Conner's pills. It was almost eight o'clock, and it wouldn't matter if I went right back to sleep. On the way to get them, I checked Rosie's room. She was sleeping, sprawled all over the bed as usual, with her covers kicked off. I pulled them up and wondered how another person could look so much like me. Then I went to the kitchen. The TV was on in the living room, and my parents were there, talking.

"I told you, I don't want to talk about this now," I heard my dad say.

"You don't have the choice," my mom answered.

"You're not hearing me."

"*You're* not hearing *me.*"

"Mom??" I called from the kitchen. "Do you have my pills?" There was a second of silence. I walked into the living room.

"They're in my purse, sweetie," she said with The Smile, and went to get them. My dad picked up the clicker and began to randomly change the channels.

"I'm going to bed now. Good night, Daddy."

"Good night," he answered, and smiled without really looking at me. I kissed him on the cheek and went back to my room. My mom brought the pills in a moment later, kissed me good night, and left.

Later I realized they were in shock. It comes on its own. You don't have much control over it. I was, too — in shock, I mean — but I was also in pain, and there was even a part of me that was relieved. Is that stupid? I was relieved that we knew what it was. That we were going to do something about it. That I hadn't made it up. It was absolutely one hundred percent real.

Of course I was scared, but I was also excited to finally be turning a corner. I would start my treatments tomorrow, and then I would start to get better. No more confusion. Dr. Conner was solid, strong, and determined. I believed in her. The bigness of her was reassuring. No one would dare refuse to do whatever she said to do. Even this Cancer.

There. I'd said it. What an ugly word it was. What a bizarre feeling to know the "monster" inside me was a bunch of cancer cells, growing and growing. In more places than hurt, according to the doctors. They were in my lymph nodes. (Where the hell are your lymph nodes???) And in my lungs. And in my hips, and maybe in my back. I lay down on my bed and scanned my whole body. It didn't look any different. I stretched and moved around. It hurt. Well, it should — it hadn't been a very good body lately. It had turned into a traitor, like Jack. Hmm, another strange fact about A Crisis. Every damn thing slips right into perspective. I hadn't thought about that creep for over twenty-four hours, and now it was too late. It was almost nine o'clock, and my pills were kicking in big time.

In the morning, my parents were better. Much. Obviously they had continued to talk, and from the looks of them, the conversation had gone on most of the night. Whatever they had talked about, whatever decisions they had made, had really made a difference. They weren't any less freaked or sad. There was still a sense of anger underneath everything my dad did. But they were my parents again, not a couple of strangers. I could believe that whatever happened, they would be there — like parents are supposed to — like my parents always had.

They were sitting at the kitchen table, drinking coffee. My mom gave me a smile when I came out, a real one, and got up to get me some juice. "Better keep it light this morning, sweetie," she said. "Remember, Dr. Conner said . . ."

"I know," I replied.

"How'd you sleep?" my dad asked, looking right at me.

"Good. I like those pills."

"I hope they're not habit-forming," he said to my mom.

"If they are, we'll deal with it when we have to, William." He smiled at her, nodding. To me, she said, "I have orange, apple, or whatever this is," holding up a bottle.

"Orange, please. What time do we leave?"

"Eight-thirty."

"Are you both coming?"

"Do you want us to?" asked my dad. "We could drop Rosie off a little early."

"Yeah, I kinda do. If you don't mind." I didn't want to tell them I was getting more and more scared about the chemo. I did want to call Sam before we left.

At first I wasn't sure I should. I didn't know how she was taking this, and I didn't think I could stand it if she was weirded out like my parents had been.

"Hello, who is it and what do you want?" she answered after the second ring.

"Hi." I thought I should start out easy.

"Girlfriend," she said. "It's about time you called me. I waited up half the night. I thought about the whole thing, and I need to tell you something, straight out. This sucks. You have no business having this cancer shit, and we're just gonna hafta hurry up and get rid of it. We have things to do. Do you *comprende, mi amiga?*"

"I sure do," I said, smiling. That was my Sam.

Part Two

Sam

"Now."

"No."

"Come on, get up."

"I don't feel good."

"You feel fine — now let's move it."

"I just had chemo. I have to sleep."

"You had it three days ago — you're fine."

"Well, I can't go to Natalie's party."

"Or course you can — you go every year."

"Well, I don't want to go this year."

"I don't care what you want. You're going."

Jules lay pouting on the bed, and I opened her closet door and started going through her clothes. She was being petulant and stupid, and I was trying hard not to lose my temper.

"What fits?" I asked her.

"Nothing."

"Liar."

She shrugged. I took out a green shirt and baggy pants.

"How 'bout this?"

"Nope."

"This?" I asked, holding up a blue dress.

"I told you, nothing fits."

"I think the green," I told her. "We can always belt the pants, it's really a good color on you, and the neck buttons up high." I took the clothes off the hangers and put them on the bed. Jules kicked them off.

"Why don't you go away and leave me alone?" she whined. I was coming close to the end of my patience. I took a big sigh and picked up the green shirt.

"If I leave you alone, then you'll never go anywhere or do anything — you'll just sit around here and rot. Is that what you want?"

"Yes."

"Well, too bad, 'cause you're coming to Natalie's party. Now, just shut up for a minute and let's get you dressed."

"I really hate you, you know?"

"Uh-huh. Get dressed."

Jules knew I'd won. She started unbuttoning the jammies she had on as I went through her drawers to look for underwear. I found a bra and tossed it to her.

"I don't need that."

"Which one do you want, then?"

"I don't need a bra. I don't have any tits."

"Shut up," I told her, but I knew she was right. She had lost so much weight that she looked like a little girl.

"Put this one on," I insisted, and tossed her a stretchy dance bra. "One size fits all."

Finally she was dressed. Almost. "Okay, where is it?" I asked, looking around.

"In my bathroom."

"Shall I get it?"

"I'll get it."

She walked into the bathroom and came back holding

a white wig stand and what she called her party wig. She had one other, her everyday wig. I couldn't see much difference.

"Bring it here."

She did, and I shook it out, then held the front while she pulled the top over her head. We'd gotten quite good at it in the past month. I started fussing around the edges in the front, combing the little bit of hair that had grown back into the wig hair, making it look more natural. She stood staring at herself in the mirror. I didn't notice until I was done that she had tears in her eyes.

"I can't go anywhere, Sammie. Please don't make me."

"Honey, you look just fine."

"Don't lie. Everybody lies to me now. Don't you start."

"I'm not lying."

She pulled me around and pointed me toward the mirror. I stared at us side by side, and my heart turned over. I used to be the pale one. Now she was, with skin that wasn't quite the right color and eyes that didn't sleep.

"Okay," I told her. "So you won't win any contests."

"Thank you."

"But you're not as bad as you think."

"Worse."

"Even if you were, I'd still make you come with me."

"Look at my hair!"

"Excuse me, I did that hairdo," I teased. "Is there a problem?"

She almost but not quite smiled, and we stood together and looked in the mirror without talking. I took her hand and told her, "If you hate it, we'll leave. I promise."

"*Promise* promise?"

"Promise promise."

"All right." She tugged at her wig and then cinched in the belt another notch. I helped blouse out the top and went to get her some shoes. "I hate how everyone stares at me," she said.

"Tell 'em to go to hell."

"Right."

I brought her black boots and helped her put them on. "Well, so what if they stare," I told her. "They're stupid, and most of 'em are ugly. You know ugly people have no class." I pulled her to her feet, announcing, "There. You're done. Let's go."

That was Labor Day. Two months earlier was an entirely different story. The day Jules told me she had cancer — July 7th — the world tipped. I couldn't seem to find my balance, so I just tried to keep moving.

In the mornings, I called Sandra.

"Hi, it's me."

"Good morning, Sammie." She was always cheerful. "She's up. You want to talk to her?"

"Sure do."

"Remember to keep it short."

A sleepy-sounding Jules would get on the phone. " 'Lo, Sam."

"What's up today, big guy?"

"Chemo again."

"Good for you. You're kicking ass, girl."

"Yeah? It doesn't feel like it."

"You are. I'll talk to you tonight. I love you."

" 'Kay. Bye."

Then I'd be off to school. I was actually doing all right in history because concentrating on the lesson made the time pass and because Brooke and I would do homework together at the library after rehearsal. Of course, Rachael and Jack were still there, determined now to mess with me, since they'd been suspended for three days by Mr. Watson. They whispered about me to anyone who'd listen, interspersing their conversation with evil little side glances. I didn't notice until Brooke told me she'd heard I was pregnant. I laughed. They snubbed me obviously in front of people in the yard. I hardly saw them. Finally Rachael started saying things under her breath as I passed her in the hall.

"You're really a loser, you know?" she hissed at me one day before class. "A dumb blond bitch."

"Give it up, why don't you?" I told her.

"Oh! It's not so fun to be on the other side of a 'joke,' is it?" Rachael taunted. Just then, Jack slid up and put his arm around her, and they both walked arrogantly into the room. Brooke rolled her eyes at me, and I shrugged. If this is what they needed to do — so what. I didn't really care.

The next day, it was Jack's turn. He watched me all through the beginning of class. At break, he approached by himself, and I wondered what the plan was.

"I just heard about Julie," he said.

"So?"

"So . . . maybe it's just a rumor?"

"No, it's true." I reached into my bag and grabbed some change for the vending machine. I did not want to discuss anything with him. Rachael was watching us from her seat, pouting.

"She really has cancer?"

"Jack, I'm going to get something to eat." I got up.

"But how's she feeling?"

"I don't know."

"What do you mean, you don't know?"

"I — don't — know. Why don't you call her and ask?"

"Well, I could, I guess. But I was hoping maybe you'd just tell her I'm thinking of her and . . ."

I shook my head and walked away.

After class, I'd go to rehearsal. Sandra had spoken at length to Linda, so all the dancers had a pretty clear idea of what was going on. No one ever really talked about it, except to ask me how she was feeling or to announce during a dance, "Don't forget — Julie goes there."

Then Brooke and I would finish our homework, and since my mom was usually out with Bruce, I'd go to The Depot for dinner. After, I'd have a quick visit with Jules. Sometimes she was sleeping from the chemo. Other times she was up and able to talk. I kept the conversation light and left the second she seemed to get tired.

Finally I'd go home. I'd usually have the place to myself. Even if Bruce and my mom were there, they didn't seem to notice me if I left them alone. I'd slip into my room and play music until I got sleepy enough to go to bed. The next day, the rhythm would begin again.

One night, my mom was home when I got there — by herself.

"Hi, Mom," I said, dropping my books and dance bag on the sofa. "Where's Bruce?"

"He's staying home tonight."

"Oh." I headed toward the kitchen. "You going over?"

"Nope. I wanted to have a little talk with you."

My stomach tightened as I turned around.

"Okay," I said, sounding calmer than I felt. I sat down on the couch and looked at her. She settled across from me on the arm of the chair.

"I saw Sandra at the market today."

"Uh-huh."

"She told me about Julie," my mother explained. "She seemed surprised that I didn't know."

"Oh?"

"You obviously do."

"Yeah."

"When did all this happen? When did they find out?"

"Just after the Fourth."

"So you've known for two weeks?"

I nodded. She looked away and then back.

"I don't understand. Why didn't you tell me?"

I shrugged again.

"This is really not okay, Samantha. You should have let me know."

"Why?" It slipped out.

She stared at me incredulously. "Because I'm your mother. Because I've known Juliana since she was nine years old."

The world tipped a bit more. I struggled to keep everything in place.

"Can you even imagine how stupid I felt?"

"Sorry."

"I mean, this is really important."

"I wasn't trying to hurt your feelings or anything."

"I know. I just don't understand why you couldn't talk to me."

"I guess maybe I needed time to sort it through on my own?"

She paused to peer at me. "And? Are you?"

"I guess." We just stared at each other for a minute. She looked away first.

"Can I go now? I'm really tired."

"Sure." I started to get up. "No. Wait." I sat back down. "Look, if you want to talk about this, about Julie . . . or anything . . . I'm here."

I looked at her again. I wished *someone* would explain all this, but I didn't see how it could be my mom.

"Okay, thanks," I told her, and stood up.

She put her hand on my arm and smiled up at me. "I mean it, honey. I'm here for you. Always."

I smiled back — and wished like hell that was true.

Julie

I went to a psychic once, with Sam. Some friends had told us about her, and we called and made an appointment. It cost twenty-five dollars, but you didn't have to pay until after, and only if you believed what she said. We were about fourteen at the time, and we didn't have friends who had cars, so we had to walk halfway up Mount Tam to get there. She did readings at her home, a small brownish house almost lost inside the trees. We went by it three times before we found it, giggling and giddy with the adventure of it all. We hadn't told my parents or Sam's mom what we were doing, and it felt dangerous and grown-up and scary. I didn't know at all what to expect. I had conjured up mind pictures of a gypsy with jewelry and multilayered skirts. Sam said no, she'd be tall and thin and ethnic-looking, Russian maybe, or Middle Eastern. Her name was Kai.

We held on to each other as we negotiated the rather precarious walk down to the house. It was the middle of the afternoon, but it seemed all of a sudden to get darker as clouds passed in front of the sun. We clutched tighter and giggled again. When we got to the front door, Sam told me to knock.

"You do it," I replied.

"No, no, no, no . . . ," she said. "This was your idea. I don't even believe in this kind of thing."

I was about to answer when the door swung open. Kai stood there, a very small, mousy hippie girl with light blue eyes who didn't look much older than we were. She was wearing a full-length green-and-gold caftan and had long, thick brown hair braided down her back. Not a bit ethnic or exotic. Not even pretty. Sam and I looked over at each other and almost burst out laughing, right in her face. She ignored it.

"I'm sorry you had trouble finding the house," she said, without any other greeting. "Shall we start? This takes almost two hours, and you don't want to be late to your dance class. Samantha" — looking right at her — "you can go first. Juliana will be second. Please come in."

She turned, and I stole a look at Sam as we followed Kai into the house. The creeps were running up her back, too — I could tell. We had never said a thing about having to go to a dance class (which we did), and how did she know we'd had problems finding the house? I hardly noticed the inside, except that it seemed filled with plants and glass things — prisms, vases, decorations — and a rather large black-and-white completely nude photo of Kai. I made a face at Sam, and she rolled her eyes.

At a low round table in the middle of the living room, Kai sat and took out a deck of cards. We took a seat on either side of her. She shuffled the cards and held them out to Sam.

"Cut them three times," she instructed. "Lay each bunch down in front of you, starting from the left."

Sam did it, then Kai picked up the top cards, laying

them in a pattern on the table. She sat a moment, head down, hand on the cards, then spoke.

"This is your present," she said, indicating the first card. "It is not a card that in itself tells anything very definitively." She looked down, closed her eyes, and rubbed her fingers around the card. "But your vibrations are quite strong. You are in a time of change, and these changes make you feel helpless and angry. Someone, a man, I think your father, is moving away, and the relationship is blocked somehow. You're not able to let him know what you need, and you are frustrated. Another person — a woman, your mother? — is also moving away. You think it is because of you, but it is not. It is a change that she herself has to make, an acceptance that she finds difficult and may in fact never attain. I think your father has another love; this is hard for her and for you. Both of them love you, however. . . ."

"Right," Sam said under her breath. I looked over. She was completely into what Kai was saying, it was so exactly what was happening. Sam's parents had just told her the week before that they were getting a divorce. No big surprise — we'd known about her dad's other woman for months — but somehow, saying it had blown everything way out of proportion. Sam's mom had started staying out all the time, sometimes even overnight, and Sam's dad didn't seem to have any time for her. Sam stayed with me as much as she could.

Kai continued. "The hardest part is still to come. Your father doesn't know how to say it, but the new love is with child. . . ."

And she went on and on and on. Almost everything she told us eventually came true. Sam's dad did have a baby by the other woman; this was what Sam's mom already knew and was probably why she was having a hard time relating to Sam. I was really concerned that all of this would hurt my Other Self and was almost sorry we had come. Sam wasn't. She was glad to know. She told me later it made things a lot easier for her to deal with.

Then came me. Kai started to hand me the cards, then pulled them back. She looked at Sam and said, "You know, I can't see the really bad things. You could walk out of here and get run over by a truck, and I wouldn't be able to see it. Everything I tell you is just probable, not actual. It won't necessarily happen, but it could. Do you understand?" Sam nodded. She looked over at me as she placed the cards in my hand.

"Do you understand?" She held on to my hand for a second as I nodded. "Please cut the cards into three. . . ."

My reading was not nearly as interesting as Sam's. She talked about a reconciliation that would occur between me and a friend, she suggested that a boy I had been thinking about was not someone I should pursue, and that a close friend, Sam, would be leaning on me quite a bit in the near future. I was not to worry, however — this friend would in turn be there for me. We smiled at each other, Sam and I, because we already knew that was true. She told me that something I loved to do would be a vehicle for success. I knew immediately she meant my dancing. When she came to "my distant future," she looked at me for almost a full minute without talking. As if she were trying to figure something out. Then she shook her head.

"I cannot clearly read this," she said, closing her eyes. "I think it's a trip, a journey — a very long one — that you will probably be making by yourself. I don't see your parents accompanying you, and though I feel Samantha's presence, no . . . it doesn't seem as if she will be going with you, either." She was quiet for a moment, then shrugged. "That's all. It's gone now." She looked up at us. Her eyes cleared, as if she were seeing us for the first time.

"Okay, that's it. Did I tell you anything that made sense?" she asked. "I don't remember what I say."

Sam glanced at me. "You don't remember?"

"Well, maybe a sense of it. But, no, I get into a kind of a trance almost. It's weird."

"Here's your money." I held out the twenty-five dollars.

"No." She smiled at us, actually for the first time. "I don't take money for readings. It would jinx me."

"But Carol said —," Sam protested.

"I know. And if *you* tell anyone about me, you have to say it will cost twenty-five dollars, too. That way, only people who really want to know will come. Hurry now — your dance class."

We smiled at her as we got up, and Sam gave her a big hug before we left. On the way back down the mountain, Sam was mostly silent. She had been given a lot of scary information, and she needed time to think about it. Funny how neither of us realized that mine was even scarier.

"A journey you will probably be making by yourself." Kai's words came back to me the second time I lay on the bed at the outpatient clinic and had chemicals dripped into my arm. The first time, I hadn't thought about anything. I was too scared. From the moment I woke up, through the conversation with my parents, the drive to the clinic, and the whole procedure of checking in and getting the IV, I was terrified. Part of me turned into this panicked Madwoman that kept stomping around inside. Another part of me went blank — I guess for balance. The blank part was calm and coherent, adultlike, able to recognize my parents' return to parenthood and to answer all the questions a nurse at the clinic asked me. At the same time, Madwoman was screaming.

"Do you have any allergies?"

"I don't think so." (*Why don't you read the goddamn chart?*)

"Are you feeling well now?"

"Yes, fine." (*How good am I supposed to feel with cancer?*)

"Do you have any cold symptoms?"

"Not that I'm aware of." (*Didn't I just tell you I was feeling fine!?*)

Another nurse started to explain the procedure. The blank part of me looked in her direction and nodded every once in a while to show her I was paying attention. Inside, Madwoman ranted and raged, and I had everything I could do to keep from running away. My mother and father asked a few questions, calmly and easily, and the nurse answered. Explanation complete, I was shown to a changing room and asked to put on a hospital gown. The nurse waited while I did; then I followed her to my bed. My parents had to wait in the reception area until the therapy was started. Then they would be allowed back in, to make sure I was all right, and to stay with me if they wanted.

I lay down. My heart was beating faster than I thought possible. My skin was warm and clammy, and I was aware how my breathing increased its tempo. I felt the prick of the needle for the IV and a long, hot searing as it went into my vein. The nurse taped it down to my arm and then taped my arm to a board. She held her fingers to my neck and felt for my pulse. Then she put the bag of chemicals on the rack and connected it to my IV tube. I glanced over. There was a clamp on the tube, so it hadn't started. I took a deep breath. Madwoman had run and hid, and my blank self had gone to look for her. All that was left was me, and I felt little and alone. The nurse put her hand on my forehead, pushed my hair back some, and stroked my face. Her voice sounded gentle but faraway.

"When the medicine starts," she said, "you'll feel a burning. Don't worry about it — it's normal. It's just the chemicals going into your vein. After about fifteen minutes, it won't seem as bad. The therapy itself will take an hour and a half. We have you on a slow drip, and we'll monitor you carefully. If there are any negative effects, we will discontinue immediately." She smiled. "Do you have any questions?"

"Can my mom and dad come in now?"

She nodded. Before she left to get them, she turned the release on the bag. I took another deep breath and closed my eyes. I concentrated as hard as I could on relaxing, and I waited for the burning to start. It came immediately and much harder than I had expected. My arm felt like it was being slashed by razors. I understood now why they had taped it to the board. I wanted to reach over and rip the needle out —

"Hi, sweetie," my mom said as she came near. I looked up at her, and my eyes were full. I didn't want to cry, but the burning didn't give me any choice.

"Hurts, huh?" she asked.

Nodding, I could hear my dad talking to the nurse.

"Are you sure this is normal?" he asked with a don't-mess-with-me note in his voice. "Look at her. She's not a wimpy kid. She doesn't cry easily. Would you please look at her?!"

The nurse answered him in a low, mellow voice, walking him back to the waiting room as she talked. You could tell she was good at calming people down. He joined us again a minute later but didn't stay. I guess he couldn't stand to look at me lying there, crying with no sound, and not be able to do anything to help.

An hour and a half seemed like days. I don't know where the nurse got her information, but the burning did not stop, not even a tiny bit. By the time the needle was removed, I couldn't even feel it. I didn't feel anything then, except more tired than I had ever been in my life. My head had turned mushy and my mouth was dry and I was definitely nauseated. I kept taking deep breaths, to try to get some normal feeling back in myself, but it didn't do any good.

I was only vaguely conscious of what was going on around me. I knew my mom was there and that some man I didn't know was helping her walk me out, and I was aware of my dad taking his place and picking me up. Then we were in the car, and I thought it would take forever to get home, even though the clinic is only about fifteen minutes away. Finally we were there, and my dad carried me into the house. I couldn't wait to lie down. Nothing in the world sounded as good right then as sleep. He put me down on my bed and that was it. I was out. I slept all the rest of the day and all night long.

• • •

When I woke up, I had no sense how much time had passed. I thought it was a few hours later on the day of therapy. I was still tired, but more like I had been dancing than taking chemicals. My arm hurt where the needle had been, and there was a red burn marking the initial chemical contact. I knew I should be hungry, and I almost was, but I couldn't think of anything that would taste good. I was just starting to try and rouse myself to get up when my mom came in with a tray.

"How're you feeling?" she asked with her mom face on.

I didn't yet realize how much I would come to hate that question.

"Pretty trashed," I told her. "What time is it?"

"Oh, a little after eight," she answered. "Would you like some breakfast?"

"Breakfast?" I was confused. Then I thought maybe since I hadn't eaten breakfast, she wanted me to eat some now. Like it was a nutrition decision or something. She realized what had happened.

"Sweetie, it's morning."

"What?"

"It's the next morning. You had the chemotherapy yesterday."

"I slept all this time?"

She nodded. "Dr. Conner said it would probably knock you out."

"Mommy . . . ," I started, feeling a rush of anger and frustration hit me. "How can I have slept all that time and not know it? And how come I still feel so bad?"

She didn't answer. She set down the tray and bundled me up in her arms. She sat with me on the bed, rocking and stroking my hair. I started to relax until I realized the worst thing.

"I have to go back tomorrow, huh?"

The second therapy was in some ways much easier than the first. I knew what to expect. I wasn't scared, as much, and I thought I was more ready for the pain. What I wasn't ready for was the isolation that settled around me about halfway through. My mom was talking, telling me stories about myself when I was a kid to try and keep me entertained, and I was watching her face as she talked. All of a sudden, it hit me. No matter how much she wanted to help, no matter how much my dad or Sam or any of my other friends or family thought they could be there for me, I was on my own. This was my journey . . . the long solo trip that Kai had told us about. I was alone, really and truly alone. I started to laugh a little. I didn't know what else to do. My mom thought I was responding to her story, and smiled.

My mother hung around the house for about a week, waiting for me to talk to her. Actually, a part of me wanted to, but where would I start? It was too weird. She'd never asked me what I'd felt about the divorce. She never wanted to hear how I was missing my dad. How could I sit down and pour out my feelings about Jules? Then, one afternoon, Sandra knocked at the door.

"Hi — sorry to barge in without calling," she said.

"That's all right," my mom assured her. "Come on in." I heard them from the kitchen and stayed there to listen.

"I wish I could, but Julie's in the car. We stopped by to invite you for dinner next Friday."

"Oh, that's sweet of you. I'll call Sammie."

"Actually, Jackie, we'd like you both to come. If you can. William's cooking. We're celebrating the end of the first month of Julie's chemo."

"Oh. Well, um . . . how nice. I'll have to check my book, of course, and see what Sammie's doing and —"

Julie honked the horn. Sandra smiled. "Sorry, better go. Give me a call and let me know. We'll eat around seven."

I came around the corner as Sandra was pulling away in her car. My mom was leaning on the closed door. She saw me, shook her head, and crossed to the sofa to sit.

"Sandra wants us to come to dinner."

"I heard."

"Do you want to go?"

"Sure. Don't you?"

"I don't know. It might not be such a good idea."

"Why not?"

"Well, Sammie, for one thing, they're *your* friends. I wouldn't know what to say to them."

"The same things you say to Bruce's friends when you go to dinner with them."

"Not hardly."

"Fine. Then don't go."

"But I want to be supportive of you."

"Then go."

She looked at me with her don't-you-understand-anything look. "I'm not sure you're comprehending the entire situation here."

"What do you mean?"

"Julie has cancer, Sammie."

"You're kidding. Really?"

"Don't get sarcastic, please. I'm trying to help you see the larger picture."

"Mother, Sandra invited us to dinner. Just dinner. If you want to go — great. You'll like it; William's a good cook. If you don't want to go — that's fine, too. It's no big deal."

"Obviously it is to Sandra." She sighed.

"Sandra will be fine. Why are you stressing?"

"Because . . . oh, forget it. You wouldn't understand."

"Try me."

That stopped her. She glared at me like it was my fault she couldn't make her point, and stood up. "Well, I'm not going to dinner there," she announced, and went into her room. She spent the evening with Bruce, and by the time Jules's celebration dinner rolled around, she'd obviously forgotten her offer to "be there" for me.

That Friday, an hour before I was due at Jules's, I came home from rehearsal, exhausted and exhilarated. I had finally mastered "The Blues Suite," Linda's new jazz/modern solo, done on pointe to a medley of haunting blues songs. I danced it around the living room, loving every step, not caring one bit that my feet were killing me. My mom had already gone to Bruce's, and I blasted the music over and over and over. It was awesome. Finally I jumped into the shower, slipped on a dress, and managed to make it over to Jules's house on time.

William answered the door.

"You look lovely," he announced, toasting me with the glass of wine he held in his hand. "Come on in. The girls are still primping. You know how girls are!"

"Yep." I smiled a little as I followed him into the living room. William is like my mom — after the second glass of wine, he becomes a completely different person. He was usually not this talkative.

"Well, it's been a hard month, but we've made it through, haven't we? I'd offer you a glass of wine to celebrate, but, well . . ." He chuckled a little.

"No problem."

Rosie came scampering around the corner in a mint green party dress, then saw me and detoured behind her father's legs. She looked taller than I remembered. I realized I hadn't really noticed her all month.

"Daddy, I wanna watch TV."

"Rosie, we have company. No TV tonight, remember?"

A storm cloud settled around her face. She threw me daggers with her eyes and plopped herself on the couch, pouting.

"How about some refreshments?" William asked.

"Creamed soda, creamed soda . . . I want creamed soda!" Rosie chanted, making an immediate recovery.

"Cream soda sounds good for me, too, thanks."

He went to get the drinks, and I sat down on the couch by Rosie. She glared at me for a minute and stuck her tongue out. I laughed at her.

"What'd I do, shortie?"

"DON'T TALK TO ME."

"I will if I want."

"No, you won't."

"Yes, I will."

"No, you will not." She held her hands up, karate style. "I will kill you."

"Oh, yeah?"

"Yes. I will kill you very very dead."

I started inching closer, moving my fingers like spider legs. "And what if the tickle bugs get you first?" She screamed and I pounced and our tickle fest began. We came up for air a few minutes later, and she tried to get her pout back.

"You better not tickle me," she proclaimed as she conveniently presented herself for grabbing. A second later we were at it again. William came back with the sodas, and Sandra joined him. They watched us, smiling, as Rosie and I finally stopped wrassling and cuddled on the couch.

"I'm glad you could come, Sammie," Sandra said, taking the drinks from William and handing them to us.

"Me, too. Sorry about my mom." I looked behind her. "Where's Jules?"

"Well, she's having a little trouble getting herself together, I think. She's still wiped out from yesterday's chemo."

"She will be joining us, though, right?" William asked.

"As far as I know." They exchanged one of those husband-and-wife looks you're supposed to ignore.

"So what are we having?" I asked.

William preened a bit. "Swordfish — broiled in lemon and garlic butter; baked potatoes — with my special secret sour cream sauce; broccoli à la William; and, of course, chocolate chip ice cream pie for dessert."

"I made the pie," Rosie bragged.

"You helped," William corrected. He looked at his watch and then at Sandra. Just then, Jules called out from her room.

"Mom??? Could you c'mere for a minute?"

"Want me to go?" I asked.

"No, let Sandra," William answered, and then spoke directly to her. "Dinner is almost ready, you know."

"I know."

"You can't let swordfish sit around for a long time."

"I understand, William."

"Hey . . . ," he said to me, "how about you two go set the table?"

"Consider it done." I grabbed Rosie's hand and pulled her with me to the kitchen. I was more at home in their kitchen than mine, and started handing stuff to Rosie to put on the table. William and Sandra lingered, whispering, and William joined us a minute later. Pouring himself a new glass of wine, he fussed around the kitchen as we finished setting the glasses and napkins. With a flourish, he transferred the sizzling fish to a serving plate, garnished it with a bit of fresh parsley, and laid it lovingly in the center of the table. Rosie peered at it carefully, and then stood back, crossed her arms, and challenged her father.

"Okay. Where are the swords?"

We were still laughing when Jules and Sandra came in. Rosie's clouds descended again, and she stared at her sister warily as they both took their seats at the table. I slid into my usual one next to Jules and gave her a little kiss on the cheek. She managed a weak smile, then lowered her eyes. I looked around the table. Rosie was still pouting, William was smiling, and Sandra just looked tired.

"To our Julie," William announced, holding up his wineglass. I picked up my water glass and held it aloft. Sandra grabbed hers, and Rosie reluctantly took hers.

"Julie?" said William. Julie threw him a look I couldn't quite decipher and raised her glass an inch off the table. William smiled and made the toast: "To Julie, for her courage and her strength. Congratulations, honey — you've got the first month behind you. May it all be over soon."

We drank, and William took my plate to begin serving.

"Mommy, may I be excused?" Julie whispered.

"Well, sure —," Sandra began.

"Honey, this dinner is for you," William interrupted.

"I know, but I can't eat it."

"Try a little," William continued.

"I don't want any."

"Now, Julie, we've talked about this before. It's important that you keep up your strength."

"I can't eat it."

"William, please," Sandra said.

"I really can't, Daddy."

"Just a little," William insisted, and put a piece of fish on Jules's plate, setting it down in front of her. She shook her head and left the table. I started to get up, too, but Sandra touched my arm.

"I'll go, Sammie," she said, and followed Jules into her bathroom. Before she shut the door, we could hear the sound of retching.

William got up to bring the tray of baked potatoes to the table. "They're hot," he warned as he served Rosie and me.

"Food makes Julsie sick now," Rosie explained, glancing at her father before confiding, " 'cause she has a big foma inside of her."

"Lymphoma," William corrected. "Sammie?" He offered a bowl of sour cream. I ladled some onto my potato. "And Rosie." He put a small dollop on hers. Sandra came back and sat down. William plopped a potato on her plate and held out the bowl of sour cream. She served herself.

"Is Julie all right?" William asked.

"She'll be fine. She's resting."

"You have to be quiet when she's resting," Rosie warned me. "You can't be loud and play. And you may not watch TV."

I smiled at her and nodded that I understood. Then I looked at both William and Sandra. They were eating quietly. "Um, do you think I should come back some other time?"

"Don't be silly," William said.

"This is all just part of it, Sammie," Sandra continued. "She'll feel better in a little while. You can take her a potato or something after dinner."

"So what have you been up to, young lady?" William asked. "How's summer school? How's dance?"

"Oh, you won't believe it," I said. "This new dance of Linda's is so awesome, and so hard, and so amazing. And I did it! I actually did it!"

"Good for you!" William toasted me with his glass.

"Thanks. I may even get a chance to perform it. I mean, I'm not that great at it yet, but I'm really working hard."

"Which dance is it? Have I seen it?" Sandra asked.

"I think so — it's the one to the music by Billie Holiday."

"Oh, yes, 'The Blues Suite.' I remember Julie telling me about it."

"Oh. Yeah, well, it was really supposed to be her dance," I explained. "I mean, she's the one who could do it best. But for now, Linda's finishing it on me and Colleen."

"You'll do great with it," Sandra said. "You were wonderful in the Showcase."

"*I'm* going to kintergarden," Rosie announced with her mouth full. "*I* get to buy a new lunch box *and* a backpack."

The rest of the dinner slipped by. We mostly talked about Rosie, who was basking in the attention. Afterward, I took Jules a baked potato with nothing on it and a glass of Sprite. She was lying on her bed with the TV on without sound. She clicked it off when I knocked and came in.

"Sorry about dinner," she said.

"No big deal." I offered the potato. "Can you eat this?"

She made a face and shook her head.

"I don't blame you." I set it down. "Here, have some soda."

She took it and sipped a little. "I heard you talking about 'The Blues Suite.' "

"Yeah."

"Is it as good as it started out to be?" she asked.

"It's amazing."

"I bet."

"I can barely do it. You'll love it."

"Yeah, well, too bad for me, isn't it?" She took another sip. "It's yours now. Or Colleen's."

She tried to smile and couldn't quite get it right. I felt like a jerk. I plopped down next to her on the bed.

"The second you're back, you'll take it away from both of us."

"Yeah, right."

"Don't be stupid. It's exactly your kind of dance."

"Really?"

"I'm afraid so."

She smiled for real. "I can't wait."

I smiled back. "Bitch."

☾

Julie

Early the next week, I had to check into Campton Medical Center in San Francisco to have a shunt put in my upper chest. The kind of "aggressive" chemotherapy Dr. Conner had me on would shut down the veins in my arms within another week. To keep this from happening, she would make a semipermanent opening and insert a shunt, a tube that went directly into my vein from the outside, which would then be used to attach the poisons.

I had stopped thinking of them as chemicals. They were poisons, pure and simple. Chemo was no more than people filling me full of poisons that could kill me, then, just before they did, giving me an antidote. In the meantime, hopefully, the poisons would kill the cancer and everyone who was still alive would live happily ever after.

The shunt sounded nasty to me, but I could accept the reasoning behind it, since my arms were already beyond pain. As long as I had to have this happen, I might as well make it as easy as I could. I surprised myself with the way I was able to put everything into perspective and how well I was managing to stay positive about the treatments. True, I hated having them and I resented being unable to function for two days after each one. But it was okay —

it really was. It was going to make me well, and then I could get on with my life. Besides, when I was sleeping, nothing hurt. And that's what the chemo made me do most of the time.

In Pre-Op, I waited patiently while the nurse tried to find a vein to give me the anesthetic. She finally settled on my hand, put in the needle, almost . . . and then had to try again on the other hand. She was arrogant the first time, shaky the second. But she got it done, and I was on my way.

When I woke up, Dr. Conner was there. Where she had put the shunt was bandaged still, but she showed me the area with a mirror. We were alone in the room.

"I want you to know something, Juliana," she said in her straightforward manner. "We are going to fight this cancer all the way."

I nodded and tried to smile, but I was still a little woozy.

"We can do it," she continued. "You're young and I'm stubborn, and we can lick it."

I drifted off, thinking it was good she was so adamant and appreciating her confidence in "our" success.

It did make it easier to go to therapy with my doctor so obviously in my corner. And with the shunt in place, getting the chemo didn't hurt as much. Everything seemed to be going as okay as this kind of thing can. Then my hair started to fall out.

It was the middle of week number five. Ten o'clock on the evening of a non-chemo day. I was feeling as "good" as I ever did. I had slept a lot that day and had even managed to have Sam over for dinner. As usual, I could barely stand the smell of it, but — unlike my "celebration dinner" — I managed to stay for the whole thing. After, Sam and I had ice cream in my room.

"Okay, we're planning your birthday," she announced. "Sit down somewhere."

"You're crazy — it's not till the middle of November. This is *August,* remember?" I dragged a few pillows off my bed and plopped down on the floor.

"That's only three months away. And seventeen is a big one, you know."

"Oh, it is, huh?"

"Absolutely. Give me some of yours," she said as she sat down next to me and shoved her spoon in my ice cream. "You're not a kid anymore after this, Jules. You're gonna hafta get your shit together."

"Yes, ma'am."

"Okay. Now." She left her spoon in my bowl and rummaged under my bed for a notebook and a pen. "Who do you want to come?"

"Well, it depends where we're gonna have it."

"In Sausalito. At Scoma's."

"We can't afford Scoma's! Besides, how do you know I'll be feeling good enough to have a party?"

"By November? Don't be dense. Now are you gonna help me plan this or not?"

"Okay, let's see. . . ."

We planned a huge extravaganza, and after she left, I felt inspired to put on some makeup and maybe even try on some of my party clothes. I went into the bathroom, washed my face, and went to pin up my hair. As I pushed it back from my face, it came out in my hand, a whole clump of it. I froze. I didn't know what to do. I stood there staring at this handful of hair, and then I shook it off my hand, like it was dirty or something. I looked in the mirror. I couldn't see any bald spot or anything, but then I have a lot of hair. Slowly, breathing really hard, I ran my hand through the other side. The same thing happened, but much worse. I could see my scalp. I dropped the hair. I screamed for my mom, and then I froze. I knew if I moved even an inch, I was going to throw the worst tantrum ever.

My mom came, saw immediately what was going on, and took me by the shoulders. She held me very close, and I started to shake, then to cry. As she guided me back to my room, my little sister came out to see what was going on. I had woken her with my shouting.

"Are you all right, Julsie?" she asked fearfully. It was all I needed. I went out of control.

"Get out of here!" I screamed at her. "Get out! Get out! What are you looking at?!"

"Stop it!" my mother said, whirling me around to look me in the face. "You stop it right now."

"Right, stick up for her!" I yelled. "You always do. She's always in the way, and you always take her side."

"Juliana, I'm not going to listen to you like this."

"That's because you never listen to me. You don't even care that my hair is falling out!" I started to sob.

"Julie . . . sweetie, I want you to sit down on your bed," she said in a soothing voice. "I'm going to talk to Rosie for a minute, and then I'll be right back."

Rosie had burst into tears of course and run back into her room. She didn't understand what was going on at all these days, except that her sister slept all the time. And now she was being screamed at by the Wicked Witch. I felt bad even then, but I was overpowered by what was happening to me, to my hair, and I couldn't find room to think about it. My mom calmed her down and got her watching *101 Dalmatians,* then came back in to me. I was sitting on my bed, staring at my dresser mirror.

"Dr. Conner said this would probably happen," she reminded me.

I nodded, still staring.

"There's nothing we can do about it. It's another thing you're going to have to find a way to live with."

I nodded again.

"I've already ordered a wig. A really good one. No one will be able to tell."

"Okay."

"Come and lie down."

I felt empty now and did what she said. She helped me undress and slip a nightgown over my head. I felt like a little girl again and wished everything could go back to when I didn't have to worry about stuff. I slid under the covers. My mom stroked my face, and I closed my eyes.

"Babygirl . . . ," she said in a near whisper, "I know this has been hell. We both know it isn't near over. I want to say that I'm proud of you. You are courageous and positive and stronger than anyone would've believed possible. You're amazing. I know you can handle this. I'm not sure how, but I know you will. I'll help whenever I can."

I started to cry. I wasn't sure why, if it was because of my hair falling out or what my mom was saying. I couldn't put it together. She reached for my hand. I looked at the lines in her face and how her eyes looked tired and old, and I knew how hard this was on her, too.

"I'll tell Rosie I'm sorry," I said. "I didn't mean to hurt her feelings."

"I know, sweetie. Go to sleep."

The next morning, huge hunks of my hair were on my pillow. My insides turned to ice. I made myself gather up every strand, and I put it in a pile on the side of my dresser. I ran my hands through what was left, and more, but not all, came out. I took a slow, deep breath and put it with the rest. Deliberately, I made myself turn and look in the mirror. A demon-girl was staring back at me, face set and cold, clumps of hair sticking out from the patches of bald.

I am not going to cry, I am not going to cry, I kept thinking, and suddenly realized I was saying it out loud. My mother opened the door. She looked and nodded.

"I brought you a scarf. I'll make an appointment with Susan as soon as the shop opens. We'll pick up the wig today."

"I have chemo," I told her.

"It can wait until this afternoon." She came over and quite deftly tied the remaining bits of hair into the scarf. It looked funny, but it was better than before.

"Breakfast is on the table," she said, and left.

I looked at the "me" in the mirror and thought about Sam's birthday plans. No way would I have a party now. Then Jack popped into my head. I could see him standing with Rachael, both of them staring at me with horrified expressions.

That's when I decided I wasn't going to see anyone until this was all over, not even Sam.

Sam

I stood looking in the mirror and tried to imagine what losing all my hair must be like. I couldn't do it.

Jules wouldn't let me visit after it happened. She'd tell me she was resting or had to go to chemo, or she'd have her mom call her away from the phone. Then she started putting on her answering machine and not calling me back. This went on for six days in a row. On the seventh day, when I knew she didn't have chemo, I didn't bother calling first. I just went over. Jules saw me parking my car and locked herself in her bedroom. She told her mom not to let me in.

Sandra did, of course, and I knocked on Jules's bedroom door. Hard.

"What?" she answered.

"Open up, Jules," I ordered.

"No way. Leave me alone."

"Grow up, would you?"

"What did you say?"

"What's the big deal? Am I your best friend or not?"

"If you were, you'd go away!"

"What if I don't want to?"

"Sam, I don't want to see you. Go home."

"Not a chance."

"I hate when you act like this."

"Well, then, open the door."

"Won't."

"Better."

"Bitch."

"Asshole."

There was a pause. I thought I almost had her and looked over at Sandra with a thumbs-up. She shook her head, disagreeing. A second later I heard the television. It was *The Young and the Restless.*

"Are you watching soaps, you idiot?" I called.

"Can't hear you — I'm watching TV," she called back.

I tried a threatening note in my voice. "Jules . . ." She didn't answer. "Jules!" Still no answer. "Juliana Elise Michaels, you open this door right now."

"Sorry, I can't play now. Maybe tomorrow."

"Jules, if you don't open the door, I'm gonna kick it in."

"You wouldn't dare. My mom'd kill you."

I looked over at Sandra, who smiled and shrugged. I kicked the door, hard.

"Stop that!"

I kicked it again, harder.

"What, are you crazy? I told you, my mom —"

"Your mom's right here."

I kicked it one more time. She flung it open, stared at me for a second with definite hate in her eyes, then walked away and plopped herself in front of the TV. Sandra gave me a look of encouragement and quietly went into the other room. I took a few steps in.

"I hope you're happy," Jules said.

I didn't answer. I was too busy staring. Seeing her without hair, with just a scarf she had tried to tie around her head, was really strange. I thought of concentration camp survivors, kids with leukemia, and really stunning models who shave their heads. I sat down, still looking.

"You could at least stop staring so hard."

"I have to look," I told her.

"Oh, right. Well, whatever *you* have to do, go right ahead. 'Scuse me for living."

"Grow up, will you? It's just hair."

"Easy for you to say."

I sighed, trying to figure out how to explain it.

"Jules, I have to make it be normal for me," I finally said. "Otherwise there'll be a wall and I can't be your Other Self. And you won't be my One and Only."

Jules made a little face, but she heard me. After a minute, she untied the scarf and pulled it off.

"So look."

I did. I looked at her head — front, side, and back. It changed a lot, not having hair, but it wasn't all that bad. Her eyes, almost black now because she was angry, seemed huge. She stared at me defiantly, not looking away for a second. I examined her for another few seconds, then shrugged.

"It's not that big a deal, you know."

"Maybe not from where you're standing." She reached for her scarf and tied it clumsily. I took it off and did it right. I could feel her shoulders stiffen.

"Really, Jules, I thought you'd look like Zombie Girl or something. You just look like you, without hair. Think of all the models who shave their heads."

"Wow, now I feel better."

"You're still pretty."

"Right."
"You are."
"Sam, I'm the one on drugs."
"Shut up. Why don't you buy a wig?"
"I bought one."
"Well, get it."
"What?"
I pushed her. "Get the damn wig and let's put it on."

Julie

Sam was the only person besides my mom that seemed to be able to remember I was still Juliana. Whatever happened, I was her One and Only. She treated me like she always had. Which was great, except when she wanted me to do something I didn't really want to do. Like Natalie's party. She thought it would be good for me, and try as I might, I couldn't change her mind.

It wasn't that the party, itself, was any big deal. Natalie had the same party at the beginning of every school year. What I couldn't handle was the fact the whole summer had gone by and the only thing I'd done was chemo. Plus I was still scared of how people would react. When I went to school to pick up my schedule and see if I'd be allowed to attend part-time, the experience wasn't exactly wonderful. I felt self-conscious about the color of my skin and the way my clothes fit. I was afraid my wig would slip and no one would tell me. And I didn't know who'd been told and who hadn't, outside of the dance company, or what I was supposed to say if someone asked.

"So you've got cancer, I hear," Mr. Heller, the biology teacher, said, taking the reality approach, showing us both *he* was together enough to say it right out loud. "That's really hard." Then he nodded, this doesn't-life-suck-but-we're-all-in-this-together kind of nod. My tenth-grade English teacher blushed and went the other way. My French teacher smiled and smiled and smiled until I thought her mouth would break. Mr. Lipton was clueless. "We missed you this summer," he informed me, patting my shoulder. "Heard you were feeling a bit under the weather."

To make my day complete, Jack and Rachael came out of the administration building, just as I was going in. He almost panicked.

"Oh. Hi," he said.

"Hi."

"Wow, we were just . . . I mean, how are you?"

"Fine."

"Oh. Good. I'm glad. Oh, you know Rachael?"

I laughed without meaning to, and they looked confused as I walked away. Sam had avoided telling me anything about them after her little escapade with the dean, and I suddenly realized I hadn't asked. So why was my stomach fluttering? Was I still in love with Jack? Thinking about it as I walked down the hall, I had to be honest. I wasn't. I didn't want him back. But I did miss being in love. We'd had some pretty amazing conversations after his dad had died and we'd gotten really close. It hurt to think he had that now with Rachael.

The final meeting, with my adviser and Mr. Marshall, the principal, finished me for good.

"You missed your eleventh-grade finals, and you can't manage the senior academic workload. I don't know what else to tell you, Juliana. You'll have to repeat the entire year," Mr. Marshall said.

"What if she comes part-time? And makes the rest up

later in summer school?" my adviser asked. "Could we waive some of the requirements and let her graduate with her class?"

"I'm sorry — I have to go by policy. You could petition the school board."

My adviser looked at me with a little smile. "We're on your side, Julie," he assured me. "But rules are rules."

Yes, I thought, and chemo is chemo. Didn't anybody get it?

I left feeling completely alienated. Climbing into my car, I thought about hitting Highway 101 and letting it take me wherever it wanted to go. North past Santa Rosa, Redding, Eureka . . . if I never stopped driving, and I never got to a destination, then I wouldn't have to have chemo; I would be done with cancer, and I would live happily ever after. Not.

I told Sam about the day on the phone, and she started cooking up the idea for us to go to Natalie's party. Of course she didn't tell me until she came over that weekend, on the night of the party. She had some stupid idea that the more I got out, the easier it would be for me. She got me dressed and ready, and I have to admit, I really didn't look so bad for a 102-pound weakling. Dr. Conner had given me a few days off of chemo, so I even felt pretty good. I decided to hell with it. What could these people do to me that the doctors hadn't already tried?

We got there early, around nine. I didn't have much stamina, so the plan was to stay about an hour and split. I was shaking as I walked from the car to Natalie's front yard. Desperately wanting everything to be the same as it used to be, I tried to find that place inside that used to make me surge with confidence. It wasn't there.

"I feel stupid," I told Sam.

"Well, stop it."

"Oh. Okay. Simple as that?"

"Heads up, cutie. Here we go."

We walked around the side of Natalie's house to her backyard, where the pool and the party were. It seemed like everyone we passed gave me the once-over. Some would smile; some just looked. People I didn't know wouldn't give me a second glance until someone I did know leaned over to tell them who I was. I wondered if this was what it felt like to be a celebrity. Leaning in toward Sam, I whispered to her.

"Do you *promise* that you would never let me go somewhere looking funny or stupid?"

"I promise."

"So why is everyone staring?"

"Because they probably don't know anybody else who has cancer."

That stopped me for a minute, coming from Miss Smart-Mouth. I laughed. She was absolutely one hundred percent right. That's all that was going on. I would've stared, too, had it been somebody else. Nobody meant me any harm. They were just curious. Smiling a little, I looked over and saw half the dance company coming my way. Strutting. They were beautiful, and they all looked healthy. Funny how you don't notice things like that when you are, too. They were in definite Company Mode. Half the time they don't like to be identified as a group, but this was different. Being in the company was their connection with me, and since I was obviously the night's main attraction, why not use it?

Colleen, tall and lanky and dark-haired with ivory white skin, started the conversation. All of them focused on me and practically ignored Sam. I wondered what it was like for her in rehearsal.

"God. You're so thin. I hate you!" Colleen said.

"You look great in that color," Sarah added.

"It's good to see you guys," I said, meaning it. Except for my brief trip to school, it had been months since I'd seen anyone but my family, the doctors, and Sam, and I was finding myself very happy to be out. Sam had been right, once again.

"When are you coming back to Company?" Brooke asked. "You're missing some awesome choreography. You should see the blues piece Linda's doing on Sammie."

"Shhh. God, Brooke," Thea chided.

"No, it's okay," I told them. "I don't know when I'm coming back. It depends on how well the chemotherapy works, and it's too early to tell."

All of a sudden it was quiet, and a thick gooey layer of uncomfortable fell over the group. It was like watching a movie where all of a sudden the camera zoomed everybody half a room away. No one seemed to know what to say or if they should say anything at all. I felt like I had just told a dirty story to somebody's grandmother. Sam snorted and shook her head.

"Lighten up, people," she warned. "What's your problem? What did you think they treat cancer with — extra-strength Tylenol?"

The girls smiled, still uncomfortable, but not so far away. One or two glanced at my head. I knew they were trying to figure out if it was my own hair. I also knew they wouldn't dare to ask.

"Well, you look fine," Brooke said. "And Linda is doing an amazing dance. You should be in it."

"I'd like to. I just can't, yet," I said. "But I'm getting better, and nothing lasts forever, right?"

Almost in a chorus they agreed with me, then seemed to somehow disappear. I could never figure out parties, how people actually end one conversation and go on to a whole new group. Now I realized that conversations aren't ended; people simply walk away. More or less. Once again Sam and I were solo. We looked at each other, and I shrugged.

"Was I okay?" I asked her.

"What, are you auditioning?" she countered.

"No, but I would like to think I didn't make a fool of myself."

"You were fine."

"Should I not have mentioned the chemo?"

"Jules, honey, they probably already know more about what you're doing than you do."

"Well, it was nice to see 'em."

"Mmm-hmm. You want something to drink?"

"Coke or Sprite, maybe. Not diet."

"Wait here."

While Sam went off for drinks, I thought about the girls in the company. I guess I was as close to them as I was to anybody at school, except Sam, of course, but I was beginning to realize that I didn't know them. Not really. I knew their names and their faces and what they would probably do in a number of different situations. I could tell you who would cry at a sad movie, maybe. But if my life depended on it, I couldn't have said what they thought about late at night, how they felt about themselves, or what they wanted from their lives. They knew even less about me, because they probably thought they knew it all.

There I was again, right back to my solo journey. Like when I started chemo, like when I found out about having cancer, like when I first looked at myself in the mirror without any hair. Sam came back with the drinks.

"I want to go," I told her, taking mine.

"We're gone."

Sam

Jules was moving away from me. I could feel a tiny space growing between us, even though I tried to ignore it. So much stuff was happening that I couldn't help her with, that she wouldn't even talk to me about. All I could do was hope we'd stay connected.

The night we left Natalie's party, she asked if we could go somewhere to look at the sky, so we drove out through Sausalito, winding around and through to the other side. Past the town, along the bay, and out by the forts that the government built during World War II, when they thought the Japanese were going to attack. Under the Golden Gate Bridge, and through a long tunnel in a hill that supports the highway up above. Coming out the other side, the real world goes away. No street lamps, no cars, no people — nothing.

Parking along one of the empty bluffs, we could watch the sky and the stars without competition from human lighting. We could look down on San Francisco Bay, over at the Golden Gate Bridge, and to the city itself.

"Want some music?" I asked her.

"No."

"Air? I can put the windows down."

"It's okay."

I settled back in my seat. I knew she'd talk if she wanted to. We watched the city sparkle and the stars burn holes in the dark. The bay waters were black and ripply, and the fog was just starting to lace itself around the bridge, sending us into a time warp where nothing was concrete or real. We sat a long time, drifting in the quiet. Finally Jules spoke.

"Do you think there's life after death?" she asked in a soft, low voice. I looked over at her before answering. I'd never heard her sound like that.

"I don't know. I mean, I guess I haven't thought about it much."

"I think there is."

"Yeah?"

"Mmm-hmm. Well, sometimes, anyway. Like right now, sitting here in the dark."

"Hm. I thought you didn't believe in God."

"I don't."

"Well, how can there be life after death if there's no God?"

"I don't know. I'm not sure." She paused, turning to look at me before continuing. "I think maybe there's a level of awareness you go to, a kind of evolution of knowing things that doesn't exist when you're alive. But God doesn't have anything to do with it. It's just . . . I don't know, the universe or another dimension, something like that."

I thought about it for a minute.

"So when you die, you don't really die . . . you just go to another dimension?"

"Well, your body dies, of course. But that other part of

you, you know, like the part that makes you who you are, your soul or something . . . it goes into this different reality."

"Okay, I think I'm following. But when you, or it, or whatever, is in this other dimension, do you know who you are? I mean, if I was there, would I know who I had been when I was alive? Would I remember me?"

"Yeah, in a way. You'd have a sense of it, of yourself, and your life. Maybe not of your whole life, specifically, but you'd definitely know who you were. For sure."

"Good."

"Until you come back. Then you'd forget the old you and have to deal with the new one."

"Why would I do that? I mean, if I'm in this other dimension, why would I want to come back here?"

"I guess to get it better the next time around. To pay off karma or learn lessons or something."

"Reincarnation."

"Mmm-hmm, and each time, in between, in that other reality, you'd know what you had to do in the next."

"And you just go on and on, keep coming back again and again?"

"Well, yeah, until you don't have to come back anymore."

"What do you mean?"

"Well, after you've learned everything, then you don't have to be here, in this reality. You get to stay where everything's peaceful. But you have to earn it."

"How do you earn it?"

"I don't know. I don't know what I'm saying. I'm just talking."

We got quiet for a moment.

"Were you okay tonight?" I finally asked her.

"Yeah. It was fine," she answered. "I suppose they were only trying to be nice."

"I suppose. They've been a little strange about it all at rehearsals. Scared to ask anything, I guess, and at the same time, really curious. You know, like last Saturday . . ."

Jules wasn't listening. She was staring out at the water. Her face was shadowed and dark, and when she finally spoke, she didn't look at me.

"Can I ask you something and you promise to answer the truth? The absolute truth?"

"What?"

"Do you think I'm gonna get better?"

The question knocked me over. I looked at Jules and my mouth was open. Anger, surprise, fear — I couldn't sort it out. I couldn't believe she was thinking it, that she would ask it.

"Why are you saying this to me?"

She shrugged.

"Of course you're gonna get better. Why are you thinking something so dumb?"

"I don't know. I didn't say it to anybody else."

"Good, it's a stupid thing to say."

"Sam, the cancer's all over me."

"So is the chemotherapy." I almost snapped at her. "Right? Am I right?"

"Yeah."

I could feel her pull back, so I tried to lighten up.

"Jules, I didn't mean to yell. But I can't believe you'd even be worrying about this. Did someone say something tonight? What happened?"

She shrugged and sat there silently.

"Do you want to talk about it?" I asked.

She shook her head. All of a sudden I got mad, not at Jules, but at the whole situation. I took her arms and turned her toward me.

"Lookit," I told her, "you are going to get better. *You are going to get better.* Are you listening?"

"Yes."

"Well, then let me say it again. You are going to be fine. However long this chemo lasts and however much your hair falls out . . . whatever happens with all this shit . . . that will not be the question. That will never be the question. Do you understand me? Am I being clear?"

She nodded and smiled.

"Say it."

"I am going to get better."

"All right, then." I let go of her arms.

"I wouldn't dare not. You'd probably kill me."

"No shit, I would. Big time!"

We started giggling, then laughing, then out and out snotty, teary, snorting laughter. We pushed and poked at each other, grabbed arms, and fell over. We finally finished and sat back, exhausted, tears still coming out of our eyes. Jules gave a big long sigh.

"I love you," she said.

"I peed my pants," I replied.

We started again, gasping and snorting, till it seemed we had no laughter left.

"I love you, too," I told her.

"I know."

Julie

Sometimes, after coming home from chemo, when I was starting to fall asleep, I'd see things. In my mind. They'd be clear and realistic, like paintings or photographs. There might be a landscape or ocean waves that came in and out, gently and without sound. There might be a person walking along the sand, or maybe a family or a dog. Sometimes there might be just a face, and even though I couldn't have said who it was, I would know it somehow — I would understand it. It might float there, flicking in and out of focus, or it might move. Often there'd be an old man, almost scary-looking, grinning at me from a corner. I enjoyed the feeling. It was like getting to open a door that nobody else could see and being let in on some kind of wonderful secret place. It was okay that I didn't comprehend what exactly it was, and it was okay if I didn't participate.

The only problem was that I couldn't ever control what happened. Sometimes, I could think what I wanted the face to do or how windy the ocean should be, and it would start happening. That was the best, like making my own movie right there in my head and seeing it at the same time. But then the face would start changing on its own, or it would disappear, the ocean would calm when I wanted it stormy, or I would realize I was trying too hard . . . or I would fall asleep. When I woke up, I would never remember the details. I would just know I had been somewhere I really liked.

I called it my Between Place, and I started looking forward to visiting there. There were never any carry-over thoughts, nothing that intruded from the other part of my awareness, my "real" self. The Between Place was protected from the rest of my day because I couldn't get there if I was thinking about it. I had to be able to relax, give up control, put myself in a frame of mind that didn't care what went on in the Outside. It was easy after chemo. I really *didn't* care.

September disappeared, and I was halfway through October before I started missing Sam. I knew she was still coming over, but I wasn't remembering the visits clearly. And I knew she still called, along with an occasional teacher and assorted people from the dance company, because the answering machine picked up the messages. I'd listen to them when I got the chance, but, except for Sam, I found it hard to call anyone back. I didn't really care who was dating whom, how hard the trigonometry test was, or who was dancing Linda's latest piece. And I was sick of being asked, "How are you feeling?"

The day before Halloween, I came down with a sore throat. My white blood cell count dropped, and I found myself back in "my" room at the hospital, hooked up to antibiotics and wishing I could escape to my Between Place. But chemo was canceled until I was better, so I was stuck with the real world. On Halloween night, all the nurses paraded through the rooms dressed as witches and monsters, passing out sugarless candy and little plastic jack-o'-lanterns. The doctor on call stopped by to check my tubing and ask me the standard questions. The TV was full of nightmare movies, so I tried to read a magazine. I wondered how Rosie looked in her Snow White costume. I thought about dancing. Finally I asked for a sedative and drifted off to sleep.

The next morning, Dr. Conner and both my parents were in the adjoining room area when I woke up. I could hear them talking and I recognized the sound of X rays being slipped into their little clips on the viewers. Pulling my rolling IV rack with me, I slipped out of bed and peered around the corner. I could see my back, my left leg, and my pelvis on the three separate screens, and I watched as Dr. Conner pointed out the dark spots here and there and spoke quietly to my parents. They were motionless. The air was absolutely still.

"Mommy?" I said, and the three of them jumped. Dr. Conner whisked the CAT scans down and back into their huge manila folder. "What are you guys doing?" I asked.

My parents faltered a bit, but Dr. Conner answered me with her usual straightforward manner. "We were discussing a possible new treatment. I have a more aggressive combination of drugs in mind. I think —"

"The cancer got bigger."

"Well, Julie," the doctor began, "let's talk about that. . . ."

"It's bigger."

"Now, Julie, listen to Dr. Conner," my dad began.

"I saw it, Daddy."

"Come on, honey. . . ." My mom took me and the IV rack and tried to steer us to the bed. I pulled back from her and looked from one to the next, ending with Dr. Conner. She stared right back.

"You're right, Julie," she said. "There has been some growth. That's why a new course of treatment is indicated. We'll wait until your white cells are up —"

"Okay, all right. Fine." Suddenly I didn't want to hear anymore. I started back to bed on my own.

"Honey, we can discuss it if you like," my mom offered.

"No, I understand. It's fine, really." I crawled back into the bed. "You know, if you guys don't mind, I'm still kinda tired. . . ."

They left a few minutes later, and I turned on the television. I didn't think about anything at all. The only thing I wanted to do was disengage. Completely.

After the new, stronger dosage was started, there was no other choice. I couldn't make decisions. I didn't have the energy to think. My hair fell out all over again, but I didn't bother wearing the wig. I went to chemo, slept, woke up, had a day or so off, and went to chemo again. I stopped listening to my phone messages. I stopped worrying about dance. I'd try to eat. I'd try to respond to my family and to Sam, when she came. Sometimes, when I couldn't stop crying, I'd try to let go and drift off to the Between Place.

One afternoon, Sam appeared in my room, dressed up and looking wonderful. I was drifting up from my Between Place and wasn't sure at first if she was really there. Then she spoke.

"Hey sleepyhead, wake up." I groaned, pulled the covers over my head, and rolled over, away from her. "Come on, you can't stay in bed all day," she went on. "It's time to party, girl!"

"Is she awake?" someone else asked. It sounded like Brooke. I opened my eyes but didn't move.

"Julie?" Still another voice. Was it Colleen? What was she doing here?

"Come on, Jules — I know you hear us!" Sam touched my shoulder gently. I snuggled farther down.

"Why don't you all wait in the living room?" I heard my mom ask. She came in and closed the door.

I uncovered myself and sat up to look at my mom. She was dressed up, too, and wore a huge grin. All of a sudden, I realized what was going on. "Is it my birthday?"

"Sure is, sweetie. You are now seventeen years old."

I ran my hand over my head. There was an uneven stubble half an inch long. "Why didn't you tell me?"

"But I did, honey. We talked about it last night."

"I don't remember!" I whined, starting to panic. "Why are they all here?"

"Sammie planned a little party for you. Just a few girls."

"Tell them to go."

"Sweetie . . ."

"No! I don't have my wig fixed. And I can't eat cake and I don't want anybody to see me. . . ."

"Julie. Julie, stop." My mom sat down with me and took my hands.

"They have to go, Mommy. Please? I don't want anybody here. Okay? Please?" I started crying and didn't see the door open and Sam poke her head in.

"Jules? Are you okay?" she asked softly. "Can I come in?"

I buried my head in my mother's shoulder. "No. I don't want you. Go away!"

"Just listen . . ."

"No!"

"Would you tell the girls it'll have to be another time?" my mom asked. Sam didn't say a word, just quietly closed the door.

One night . . . afternoon? morning? I called out, and when no one answered, I bumbled my way out to use the bathroom. Sam was there, with my mom. They were sitting in the den, having coffee and talking. I went around the corner and stood where they could have seen me if they'd looked up. They didn't. Sam was showing my mom the last of a pile of pictures.

"And this is Bruce again," she explained, "in his disco outfit." My mom laughed, and Sam joined in. It all seemed so ordinary.

"They went dancing at the casino almost every night."

"What did you do?"

"Walked around, swam at the hotel. There wasn't really enough snow for skiing yet, but it was okay. I was glad I went. Tahoe's really pretty this time of year."

My mom picked up another picture. "And who's this?" she asked with a smile and raised eyebrow.

Sam was embarrassed. "Oh. That's Paul. I met him at the hotel. He lives in San Francisco."

"He's very cute." She picked up the last one. "Oh, this is in front of your house. Okay, young lady, tell the truth . . . are the two of you an item?"

"No, not really. Well, maybe a little. I mean, we're going out. But I'm not in love or anything."

"Well, he looks like a nice guy. Does your mom like him?"

"I think so. Who can tell? I hardly see her."

"Yeah, she's had a lot to deal with. With your dad and all."

"I guess." Sam put the pictures away, and they both were quiet. "Do you think Jules might be up?" I ducked back behind the wall just as they both looked in my direction.

"I haven't heard her. She sleeps a lot with the new chemo."

"I guess that's good, huh? She'll get better sooner."

"Yep."

They got quiet again; then my mom took Sam's hand. "It's been pretty rough, huh?"

Sam nodded, and her lips pressed together. My mom put her arm around her. She looked at her with that quiet listening way she has and then pulled her in close. Sam was crying, and my mom stroked her hair. I could hardly hear the words when Sam was finally able to talk.

"I don't know what to do with myself," she said. "I miss Jules all the time. Summer was bad enough, but at least then we could talk. Now she's so . . . different."

My mom nodded. "She can't help it, Sammie — it's the chemo."

"Oh, I know. I know it's not her fault. She just seems so faraway. She's barely ever awake when I come over. And she doesn't call anybody back. And then when I do get to see her, I do all the wrong things." My mom handed her a Kleenex from the end table, and she blew her nose.

"You do fine, Sammie."

"Yeah, right. Like the birthday party. What a stupid idea."

"No, it wasn't stupid. She just wasn't up to it."

"Maybe. But you know what? I don't think she wants

to see me anymore. I'm just like anyone else to her now."

"That's not true."

"Well, it seems like it. I mean, having Paul around helps, I guess, but it's not the same. He doesn't know me like Jules does." She sighed. "Everything's so screwed up. She should have come to Tahoe with me. We always have Thanksgiving together! And now — how can I do Christmas shopping? What good is having Christmas break?"

I leaned back against the wall for support. Christmas? When was Christmas?

"You know how she is. She still believes in Santa Claus!" Sam was smiling a little now, still wiping her nose. My mom was smiling, too.

"She is a little wacky this time of year," my mom said.

"A little? She's like a big old kid. I was trying to explain it to Paul." She blew her nose. "You know — like when we were ten and she found all the presents? Remember how she . . ."

I went to use the bathroom and then directly back into bed. I could hear the two of them laughing. I tried and I tried, but it was beyond me to straighten it all out. Was I crazy? Or was it the chemo? Sam was on Christmas break, and I didn't even know when Christmas was. In two days? A week? Or had it happened already? This stupid cancer had canceled everything else in my life — had it canceled Christmas, too? I lay back on my bed, exhausted. I fell asleep feeling tears on my face.

To make it worse, I woke up at three in the morning — four days before Christmas, I found out later — with a temperature of 105. By the time my parents called Dr. Conner, bundled me up, got my grandma to come stay with Rosie, and shuttled me across the bay to Campton Medical, I was almost delirious. The shunt had allowed an infection to start in my blood stream. I spent the next few days hooked up to an IV with rivers of antibiotics being poured into my body.

Christmas Eve came and went. So did Christmas Day. I still floated in and out of it, but the antibiotics were finally doing their work and the fever had gone. I felt drained, helpless, and frustrated. My parents acted like everything was just fine.

"We'll just have to have Christmas right here," my mom announced sometime during the week. "It'll be fun." Then she brought in tinsel and ornaments and presents. She pinned a huge Santa Claus on the door, and finally she set up a small plastic tree with tiny blinking white lights. Every time I woke up, I'd see it there, smirking.

It was awful. Everyone smiled too much. I pretended I didn't see them. They pretended I was more than a pouting, pissy lump in the bed. And we all pretended we didn't hear Rosie when she put her hands on her hips and announced, "This is stupid. You're supposed to have Christmas at home."

Two days before Christmas, when I was in the middle of packing for a ski trip with my dad to Heavenly Valley, he called.

"Hi, honey. Merry Christmas."

"Hi, Daddy. You, too. When are you coming? I'm almost packed."

"Well, actually, that's why I'm calling."

I knew it. "Oh?"

"Monica has a bad case of strep. Ruthie thinks I'd better stay home."

"But Daddy, we planned this for a month."

"I know, honey, and I couldn't be more disappointed. But these things happen. You'll just have to be my big girl now. There'll be another time."

Of course, since my dad was supposed to have picked me up that afternoon, my mom had already left to spend Christmas week in Tahoe with Bruce. Paul was visiting his dad in Los Angeles. I called Jules's house. Sandra answered.

"I'm sorry, sweetie — she's back in Campton for a few

days. Probably at least through Christmas. Another infection."

"Oh, I'm sorry."

"Yeah, me, too. We're just on our way over to visit."

"Well, tell her I said hi."

"I will. Why don't you give her a call in a day or so? I know she'd love to hear from you."

I wasn't so sure. After the birthday fiasco, I'd seen Sandra several times, but Jules and I hadn't talked at all. As I hung up the phone, I wondered why Sandra hadn't asked me to go with them, then realized I was glad. I didn't want to spend my whole Christmas thinking about cancer. I called Paul's number in L.A. No one answered. I thought about going over to my dad's, but with Monica sick, Ruthie would be even worse than usual. I got bored with TV, wandered around the house, called out for pizza, and finally, out of desperation, called Brooke. She was at her parents' house in Sausalito.

"Get over here," she said, giggling. "Bring your stuff and stay the week. Everyone else is!"

The next few days were a party. Thea and Colleen were also staying with Brooke, whose parents had a huge house and were very easy to be around. Christmas Eve, we sat on the deck, watched the city lights, and drank hot buttered rum. Christmas Day, Brooke's parents had a present for each of us. It was the most fun I'd had in months. I completely forgot my disappointment about my dad. I didn't miss Paul at all. I hardly thought of Jules and never got around to calling her to wish her a merry Christmas.

That night my mother phoned. Brooke rolled her eyes as she handed me the porta-phone. I pointed to the extension in her room and waited until she had picked it up before I said hello.

"Where the hell are you?" my mother demanded. Brooke threw me a look and stifled a giggle.

"Um . . . at Brooke's house. Didn't you just call here?" I barely got the sentence out. Brooke was on the floor, laughing.

"Your father phoned last night to wish you a merry Christmas. I thought you were spending the holiday with him."

"Me, too. He flaked."

"Well, I've been out of my mind." Brooke nodded, and I shot her a warning glance. "You might at least have left a note."

"You weren't supposed to be back until tomorrow."

"Don't get smart with me, young lady. I was up all night worrying about you." Brooke made a "yeah, right" face.

"Okay. Do you want me to come home?"

"Frankly, at this point, I don't care what you do." She hung up and I looked helplessly at Brooke.

"I don't know," she said. "She's your mother."

"I better go."

I packed my stuff and was home an hour later. Bruce was there and tried his best to pretend my mother wasn't ignoring me. We sat chitchatting in the living room while she banged about in her bedroom, getting ready to go out.

"So where is that nice new boyfriend of yours?" he asked.

"Visiting his father."

"Oh, that's too bad. I bet you miss him, hm?" I did, actually, now that he mentioned it. It would have been nice to have been sitting there with him instead of Bruce. I could feel the good mood from Brooke's house starting to fade.

"And how's your little friend with cancer?"

"She's in the hospital for a few days."

"Oh, dear, that's a shame."

My mother couldn't resist. "I don't suppose you called her, either, did you?" she yelled from her room.

Everything I'd been trying not to think of circled around and smacked me in the head. I mumbled something about needing to wash my hands and excused myself. From my bedroom, I tried Paul again in Los Angeles. This time he was there.

"I miss you!" was the first thing he said. "It's really a drag here."

"It is here, too."

"You sound like you're home."

"I am. And my mom is being a real bitch."

Just then she stuck her head in my room,

"We're leaving," she said. "We'll be at Marin Joe's if you need us."

"Have a good time," I said.

"Are you talking to Julie?" she asked.

"No. Paul."

She frowned and shook her head at me and closed the door. Paul and I talked for another hour — about nothing, really, but it relaxed me enough to fall asleep. When I woke up around two, the lights were still on in the living room. My mom wasn't home yet. The house felt even emptier than usual. I was thinking about Jules, and missing her, a lot.

The next morning, I left the house before my mom woke up and drove to Campton Medical.

"I'm sorry — Julie Michaels has been placed on a 'family only' restriction," a dumpy young nurse told me.

"I know," I replied. "I'm her sister."

She gave me the once-over and shook her head. "I'm afraid there's no sister listed here," she said, checking a file and giving me a who-are-you-trying-to-kid expression.

I went all the way down to my car, got in, turned on the ignition, got mad, and reversed myself — right back up to Jules's floor. This time, I hung out by the patient's elevator until the nurse at the front desk went to answer a call. Then I snuck around the corner to Jules's room and slipped inside without knocking. She was cuddled in a little ball, facing toward the wall.

I didn't know if I should wake her. "Hey, are you sleeping?" I whispered. She didn't move, and I almost turned to go when she rolled over to look at me. For a moment, we just stared at each other. She looked a lot sicker. Then she smiled, and I took a few steps closer to the bed.

"Hi," she managed, then licked at her lips. They were pretty chapped. "Merry Christmas."

"You, too. How are you feeling?"

"I'm okay, I guess. No more infection. How are you?"

"I'm okay."

She nodded. "How was your Christmas?"

I shrugged. "No big deal." Then there was a long silence. It was hard to look in her eyes. I felt like I was shrinking.

"I didn't think you'd come."

I smiled. "Well, I wanted to," I lied, "but you're on this family restriction thing. I had to sneak in."

"I'm glad you did."

I babbled on. "So did you have a good Christmas?"

"Sure, it was swell." I ignored the sarcasm in her voice. "My parents stood around and grinned at me."

"Well, this is pretty," I said as I noticed the little Christmas tree.

"Yeah, artificial trees are my favorite."

"Well, at least they're trying to make it nice for you." My words came out sounding pretty harsh. She blinked a couple of times.

"I suppose," she said in a little voice, and turned slightly away. The silence that followed got awkward quickly. All of a sudden I was pissed.

"Well, don't worry — you'll be home soon."

"Maybe two more days."

"Hey, I better go before I get caught. Merry Christmas." I leaned down and brushed her cheek with my lips and went to the door. "I'll call you when you get home. Okay?"

I don't know if she answered. I had to get out of there so I wouldn't say something mean. Miss Dumpy Nurse saw me close the door, but I made it to the elevator before she could get to me. I rushed through the lobby and out to my car, then had to take a moment to get myself together before driving. Jules really was different. She acted like she was the only person in the world who had problems. Of course she hated spending Christmas in the hospital, but at least her parents cared enough to be there for her. At least they tried to make the best of a bad situation.

By the time Jules got out of the hospital, Paul was back and we were seeing a little more of each other. I thought of her but didn't really have a chance to call. On New Year's Eve, he and I went to a party in Larkspur, then drove up along the coast and parked. The fog came in, surrounding the car and suspending us in a patch of wispy, white-gray nothingness. I leaned against the door.

He put a mellow tape in the deck and reached for my hand. I knew he was going to kiss me, and as he did, Jules popped into my head. I pushed her out. Phone lines go both ways. If she really wanted to stay in touch, she could call me.

Two weeks later, on a Sunday, not quite seven in the morning, my mom answered the phone. She came into my room, yelling.

"I don't know who it is, but you tell your goddamn friends to buy a clock — and I don't care if it is an emergency!" Still ranting, she threw her porta-phone down and slammed my bedroom door as she walked out. I picked up my own extension, which had been turned off.

" 'Lo, whozit?" I mumbled, still half asleep.

"It's Sandra, Sammie. I'm sorry to call you this early. I've been up with Jules all night, and . . ."

I was instantly awake. My whole body changed. I was hot, then cold, then numb. I started to sweat, on my forehead, hands, armpits. My breathing went faster, my heart, too. I almost couldn't listen.

". . . I don't know what to do. I can't talk to her; she won't listen . . ."

"Sandra, Sandra . . . is she, ah, I mean, is she okay? . . ."

There was a pause, and Sandra chuckled, not the funny kind, but the way you do when you really don't expect something.

"Oh, sweetie, oh, I'm sorry. Yes, she's fine. I didn't mean that . . . no, no, she's fine."

I relaxed, laughing a little and shaking my head. Whatever the problem, it wasn't the Awful Thing. I hadn't realized until then how scary that was. It was okay now, though — I could put that thought away. Sandra went on.

"It's just that she's got an idea in her head, and she won't listen to us. William is fit to be tied. Can you come over? I need you to talk some sense into her."

"What is it? What's she doing?"

"She insists on stopping the chemo. She's adamant. Nothing we say seems to penetrate." She paused, sighed, then continued: "Sammie, that's her only hope. . . . That's the only way the doctors know . . . and —"

"I'll come right now," I said. "But I'm not all that sure she's gonna want to listen to me, either. I mean —"

"I know. Christmas was hard on us all. But you're still her best friend, you know?" (I wasn't so sure.) "Would you like me to clear it with your mom? I don't think she was too happy about the call."

I started laughing. "No, it's okay. I'll be right there."

There were no early risers in the Michaelses' neighborhood. At seven-thirty in the morning, Jules's house was the only one with lights on. It was chilly, the fog was in low and thick, and the house looked warm and safe and happy. I knocked on the door. William answered.

"Thanks for coming over, Sammie," he said after taking my coat. "I'm sorry we had to bother you so early."

"No problem."

"They're in the den." He nodded toward the other room, then put his finger to his lips, explaining, "Rosie's still sleeping."

Walking in, I noticed right off that something had changed about Jules. It wasn't just that she hadn't bothered to cover her head with a scarf. I had gotten used to seeing her like that. It was a feeling about her, an energy.

It was completely alien and yet somehow familiar. She hadn't been like this for a long, long time. Her eyes were sparkling, and her body was held proud, tensed and ready to fight. She was obviously enjoying this confrontation. She knew she had her parents cowed.

"Called in reinforcements, huh?" she teased her mom and dad, smiling at me. I smiled back, a bit tentatively.

Sandra brought me a cup of coffee. I sat down on the other end of the couch from Jules. We looked at each other, and then she winked. I smiled big.

"Last night, about ten," Sandra explained, "this young woman announces to her father and I that she's 'tired of this shit' . . . is how I believe she put it, and informed us that she's not going to do it anymore. Period. 'End of Story.' "

"The chemo?" I said.

"The 'fucking chemo' is how she described it."

"Oh." I looked over at Jules, and we tried unsuccessfully not to laugh at how strange Sandra sounded saying that word.

Sandra and William exchanged looks. When we had ourselves under control, Sandra went on.

"Now, as I explained to you on the phone, and as Julie knows quite well, the chemo is the only treatment available for the lymphoma . . ."

"Not true," Jules said very softly.

". . . and Dr. Conner feels very strongly that it is the best course to take," Sandra finished.

"First of all," Jules said, "you're wrong. Dr. Conner is wrong, too. There are all kinds of ways to treat cancer. She knows the medical way."

"Look here, Julie," William interjected. "If you're even

considering one of those crackpot treatments you get in Mexico, I've already told you, you might as well forget it. They're bunk. They take your money and give you nothing but false hopes in return. They don't work."

"What, did you watch *60 Minutes* or something?" Jules countered sarcastically.

"I won't have that tone of voice, young lady," he shot back.

"Let's not start again, okay?" Sandra asked. Everyone sat quietly for a moment. I looked down at the floor. I was caught in the middle of this family, and I didn't want to be asked what I thought. At least not until I knew. Jules pulled her robe in around her, and when she spoke, it was low and powerful, like Sandra.

"If you want me to go back for chemo, you're going to have to drag me. I'm not going on my own. I'm not giving you permission to take me."

"We don't need your permission. You're not of age." William was on a dad power trip and couldn't let go.

"Fine. Then you get a straitjacket or whatever you think you're going to need, and you find a way to get it on me before Tuesday. Because that's the only way you're going to get me there."

"Julie, please . . . ," Sandra pleaded.

"And you better tell Dr. Conner to have some pills ready, 'cause she'll have to knock me out. I'm done with it. Nobody's putting anything in this body that I don't want, and I don't want any more chemo."

"Juliana!" William was really getting angry. Sandra put a hand on his arm, and he turned away, shaking his head in frustration. I didn't know what to say or do, because I wasn't sure whose side I was really on. The room got very still, and no one could look at anyone else. Finally Jules spoke, her voice gentle and soft.

"Dad, you don't get this at all. None of you do. I'm the only one who has to be hooked up to that IV tube. I'm the only one who feels lousy and can't function, who can't do anything but get sick and sleep . . . and then get hooked up all over again."

"You're right," Sandra said. "We don't get it — there's no way we could. We do know it's hard and horrible. And we know how brave you've been in facing all of it."

Jules sighed, held a hand up.

"Stop, please. You're not hearing me at all. I'm not brave. I'm not *anything*. If I was, I might've quit this a long time ago. It was just easier this way. I didn't know what to do, so I put myself in Dr. Conner's hands. Well, I don't think she knows what to do, either. Because now I can read those CAT scans just as well as anyone else, and I know I'm not getting better."

I looked over at Sandra and William. Their silence and the expressions on their faces told me this was true. I looked back at Jules. All of a sudden I didn't feel I knew her that well. Was this my One and Only? The person who had cried at the beach over a stupid boy? It sure didn't seem so.

William tried speaking calmly. "The only person who really knows what those CAT scans mean is a doctor."

"Bullshit." Jules was equally calm. "A moron could see the dark areas are getting bigger. And there are more of them, here . . . and here," she said, touching her head and her chest. "So you can get as pissed as you want, Daddy, but it isn't going to make any difference."

William looked like he would explode any minute. Sandra had started to cry, very softly, blinking back the tears. I felt about six years old. I didn't have a clue what to say or do, so I just jumped in.

"Well, what do you want to do?" I asked her.

"Find a different kind of treatment."

"Your mom says there isn't any."

"Maybe not a medical one. But lots of people have survived cancer without medical treatment. There's a lot more out there than chemotherapy. I want to know what it is."

"What if nothing else works?"

"Then maybe I'll go back to this," she said, gently touching the shunt in her upper chest. "But not now." She looked over at her dad. "Unless, of course, they tie me down."

"I think she means it," I said to Sandra, who nodded.

"Maybe we should talk to Dr. Conner first," William said.

"Talk all you want," Jules told him. "I'm not changing my mind." She sat back, eyes straight ahead, and waited. I knew her parents were freaked, and I could understand why. But Jules was right — we didn't have to have needles stuck in us. We didn't have to feel horrible all the time. We were doing our normal life, mostly, except for worrying about her. I took a big sigh. All the anger I'd been feeling, and all the petty thoughts, evaporated. This was my One and Only.

I looked at her closely. Her baldness was part of her now. It defined her face, made her eyes huge and black and old. She had no fat anywhere; she had shed a whole outer person and was left with the core. She must have felt extremely weak. She'd had chemo on Thursday, slept most of Friday, and stayed up all night long.

And yet, I would not have tried to cross this person for any amount of money. Not at this moment. She had too much determination and too much strength. As small as she was, as fragile-looking, I believed she could do whatever she wanted. Just then, she turned to look at me. When our eyes met, I suddenly recognized her. I don't know why. She smiled. I smiled and reached out for her hand. Neatly, smoothly, the world tipped back into place.

Julie

You should have heard Dr. Conner roar. I mean, she roared. My mom and I sat back in our chairs, not knowing where to look. My dad had stayed home with Rosie. A passing nurse frowned at the noise and shut the office door. None of it fazed the doctor. She continued to rage.

"I have never in my life heard anything so totally irresponsible," she ranted. "Perhaps you don't understand what it is you're saying. Perhaps you're under the impression that we're playing games here. Doing therapy for the fun of it? What could be in your mind?" She looked hard at me and shook her head. "What could possibly make you come to such a stupid decision?"

"That'll be enough," my mom said, meaning it.

"I'm sorry," the doctor said immediately, then went behind her desk and sat down. Deliberately, slowly, trying to pull herself together. "I was out of line."

"Yes, you were."

There was a long moment of silence while the doctor considered her words. My mom took my hand.

"I'm afraid you don't understand the ramifications of your choice," she said in a quieter, calmer tone.

"I think we do."

"Perhaps not as clearly as you might."

"Dr. Conner, I feel very strongly that this choice must be left to our family. I appreciate your input. I realize the energy and work you have put into us, uh, our case, and I appreciate that, too."

"Mrs. Michaels, this is not a decision to be made lightly."

"We're aware of that."

"If Julie stops the chemotherapy, nothing will be preventing the spread of the cancer."

"We understand that."

"Obviously you don't. If the cancer spreads —"

"Dr. Conner," my mom interrupted. "This conversation is ended." She stood up; I followed. Dr. Conner came around from behind her desk.

"Very well." She held out her hand, and my mom took it, but they didn't shake. Just stood there for a moment, holding hands. "Will you keep in touch?" the doctor asked. "Will you let me know how Julie is doing?"

"If you like."

"I'd appreciate it."

"Fine."

"She should continue to come in for checkups."

"She will."

"Well, perhaps I'll see her then."

We stepped toward the door. I thought the doctor would say at least one more thing, like "best wishes" or "I'll be thinking of you," but she just stood, a soldier defeated. We left and closed the door quietly behind us.

In the car, my mom started to cry. Not a real cry — she only does that at night, if my dad's out, or when she thinks no one will hear. I'd heard her lots of times recently, when Rosie and my dad were gone and she thought I was sleeping from chemo. This was something different. A Sandra cry. Most people wouldn't even realize she was crying. Her face got dark, sort of shaded and closed, and her mouth pulled in tight. There might have been a tear or two in her eyes. But the voice would be the clue. It turned husky and down at the bottom of her range. I could barely hear her.

"I sure hope we're doing the right thing," she said.

Me, too, I thought. Me, too.

It's funny how my parents and Sam and especially Dr. Conner seemed to think my decision to stop chemo was made quickly or easily. Like maybe I woke up one day saying, "Whoa, had enough of this, dude — better move on." The truth was, I had thought of nothing else since spending Christmas week in the hospital. In those few moments I was able to think, that is. It had started after Sam's visit. I cried myself to sleep that night. The next morning, for the first time, I found myself in the Between Place as I was waking up, sitting right next to my almost scary-looking old man. I stayed there as long as I could.

My eyes were still closed when my mom peeked her head in the room a few minutes later. She watched me a minute, then whispered, "Julie? Are you awake, honey?"

I didn't answer, and she quietly shut the door. She'd walk around and come back in fifteen minutes or so. I needed the time to myself, without having to inventory how I was feeling or decide what I was going to be able to eat. That was the business of me. I was engaged in the reality.

I knew I was fully awake, and I knew that something of my other place woke up with me. Never before in my life had I felt myself so completely. My Self. A mixed-up jumble of feelings, thoughts, wishes, hopes, goals . . . a hodgepodge of happiness and sadness and anger and despair . . . of jealousy and wisdom, ignorance and knowledge. It was packaged inside a body I used to take for granted, a body that had run and danced effortlessly. It was directed by a mind that had found it easy to be witty and funny — or serious and deep. It belonged to a person that woke up each day and did it — the day, that is — without ever having to examine what exactly she was doing. My Self had simply been. I didn't know why. I had never asked. And I didn't know who she was, not really.

Now thoughts I'd not bothered to reach for presented themselves, and feelings I had been afraid to look at stood up and paraded. Never before had I been able to see Me in such a revealing way. I felt the same fascination that people drawn to a bloody car accident do. It was terrifying, and completely inescapable.

With a big *thump,* I realized that what I'd been doing for the past six and a half months, since Dr. Conner had told me about the cancer, was ignoring it. It wasn't hard. Having chemo, being in the hospital — the whole thing was like being on stage. All I had to do was show up at the designated time and lie down. (I did the lying down part, anyway — my parents were actually responsible for the showing up.) Everyone else had roles to play, and we all said our lines on cue. Nurses would be sympathetic and supportive, or professional and removed. Orderlies would joke around with me or ignore me completely. My parents got to balance between their own feelings and trying to keep me from freaking out. And friends got to be "nice" — except Sam, of course — or bewildered or confused about how to talk to me. I simply sat center stage and went along for the ride.

What else do you do when A Doctor tells you you have cancer? You Do What the Doctor Says. She Knows Best — That's What We Pay Her For — We Didn't Go to Medical School. Plus you're scared. To have a prescribed course of action and be told it must begin immediately feels like a gift, especially after all those other doctors not believing anything was wrong. Then after the therapy starts, it's so horrible that you figure it must be working.

Unfortunately I had suspected for a few weeks now that this extra-strength chemo wasn't doing what Dr. Conner had hoped. Of course, I knew it had worked for other people. I'd met them. But those dark spots on my CAT scans weren't getting any smaller. Besides, I had started out Stage Four, and all the books my mom had gotten at the library (and carefully hidden) agreed that anything past Stage Two drastically reduced the chances for "success."

It was very strange to realize I wasn't involved with my own life. As much as I still believed in Dr. Conner's desire to cure, I wondered if it really had anything to do with me. Was it possible to care about every kid you treated, or was this just another battle in her overall war? And what if there wasn't any other kind of treatment? Then I would be left with the cancer.

No journey more solo than that one, I thought, and then everything threatened to shut down. My ears closed up, my eyes throbbed, my throat filled with cotton. I could hear the blood rushing through my head. Go on, I told My Self. You can't come this far and back down now. Say it.

SAY IT.

If I was left with cancer and that cancer could not be treated, THEN I WOULD DIE.

Suddenly the hospital room went away and I was somewhere out on the clouds, soaring in absolute silence, feeling nothing and everything, not able to speak or see or hear. I must've passed out for a second, because the next thing I knew, I was sitting straight up, drenched in sweat, freezing cold, and absolutely calm.

The thought came again. I stepped back to look at it this time. I had to, knowing with more clarity than I had known anything before that I was actually considering my own death. My own death. Realizing, a split second after, that meant considering my own life. You can't be thinking this, came a voice; you're only a kid. I laughed out loud. There's nothing else to do, I answered. It *is* My Life. My Death. My Self. My Decision.

And that was the beginning. After I got out of the hospital, it took another two weeks, saving my strength in between chemo sessions, to confront My Self over and over and make sure that I was being completely honest. I read through my mother's books on cancer again. Someone had marked several passages about holistic healing. I wondered if it was she and if she was also questioning the treatment and the doctors.

The chemo scheduled on the Thursday before I told my parents I was quitting it all was a particularly rough session. I didn't want to do it. I resisted waking up; I was slow getting dressed. I didn't talk to the nurses or chitchat with the other patients. I lay there passively enough, but

I fought the needle and the chemicals and the nausea and the fatigue. It only made everything worse. I cried all the way home in the car.

"Are you in pain, sweetie?" my mom asked.

"No," I replied, irritated.

"Did somebody say something?"

"No."

"Well, you let me know if —"

"Just leave me alone, okay?" I snapped at her. It wasn't unusual behavior for me after chemo, so she didn't take particular notice. I did. I felt so much anger at myself for yelling at her. I wanted to tell her I was sorry, but I couldn't make the words. As I lounged against the car door and watched her drive, I realized she was wiped out, too, completely, utterly, the same as me. But she never yelled or bitched or took any of it out on me or my dad or Rosie. She always got up when I needed her and never complained about it being the middle of the night. She held me when I cried; she calmed me when I raged. She cleaned up after me, and she never ever asked me anything in return. I loved her so much, and she didn't even know it. The drugs rendered me incapable. I knew the moments to speak, realized what she needed to hear, but I couldn't focus enough to say it. My life was going by me, and I wasn't participating.

I sighed and stopped fighting the fatigue. When we got home, I kissed my mom and gave her a big hug before going to lie down. I immediately started drifting off, and just before I arrived at the Between Place, I knew it for sure. That was the last time. I was done with the chemo. From now on, my life would belong to me.

☼ Part Three ☾

Sam

Jules was back. I mean, the girl was *back*. It had only been three weeks since the night she proclaimed her independence from drugs, and barely two days since she and Sandra had come back from the holistic healing place. But she was already beginning to act like her old self. She still wore her wig, but she had almost an inch of new hair under it, and it was kinda cool. She looked like a French model, avant-garde hairdo and skinny skinny body. Of course she complained about not having any tits, but what else is new? She was feeling stronger, she was *there*, and she didn't have to sleep all the time. She was even enrolled in one class at school. I was going to drive her the first day back.

It was a Tuesday. She spent Monday night at my house (the first time *that* had happened in too many months!), and I tried to talk her into going without her wig.

"You look *amazing*," I argued. "You look beautiful and exotic and spectacular."

"Right."

"You do. I swear. You know I wouldn't lie to you."

"Well, just in case there are a few stragglers who didn't know I was wearing a wig . . . and just in case I decide to go back to chemo and lose my hair all over again, I don't want to have to explain how it grew from here" — she pointed at her head — "to there" — she pointed at the wig — "instantaneously. *Capiche?*"

"*Capiche.* But are you really thinking about doing more chemo? I thought you were done with all that."

"I'm thinking about everything."

"I thought you'd been feeling good."

"Yeah, I have."

"Well . . . why change anything?"

"The feeling good is kind of a reaction to stopping the chemo."

"Okay."

"It doesn't mean the cancer is going away."

"Oh. But now you're doing all that holistic stuff."

"Yes, I am."

"Well?"

"Do you think I should wear this one or this?" she asked, holding up two new blouses.

"The blue. Are you trying to tell me you don't want to talk about this?"

"God, are you quick. I always tell people, she only looks stupid."

I punched her.

Tuesday morning, on the way to school, Jules kept adjusting her wig and fixing her collar and squirming in her seat. I waited for the outburst.

"Why am I scared to go to my own school?" she finally blurted. "Can you tell me that?"

"I don't know."

"Well, I do. I don't want everybody to stare at me or

come up and ask me stupid questions or try to figure out if I'm wearing a wig."

"Okay."

"But they will."

"Okay."

"Oh, you're a big help."

"I don't know what to tell you. You've been gone practically the whole damn year."

"So?"

"So, believe it or not, people like you. They're probably concerned."

"Concerned, my ass — they're curious."

"So? Wouldn't you be?"

"Sam, you're supposed to take *my* side."

"I am."

"Great. With friends like you . . ."

"Shut up and relax, would you?"

"I am relaxed."

"Right, I can tell."

She sat back and pouted until we turned into the school parking lot, and two Company girls saw us from their car.

"Shit, there's Brooke and Colleen. Keep going, keep going," Jules urged.

"Stupid. It's my parking spot."

"Fine. See if I ever do you any favors."

They called to Jules, got out, and ran over to our car. She rolled down the window and smiled and talked, and I watched her and knew everything was going to be easy.

Which it was, right up until she saw Jack. We were coming down the stairs from the science building, laughing over something stupid someone had said in my physics class. Sandra was picking her up in about ten minutes, and I wanted to walk her to the front. Suddenly, Jules reached over and grabbed my arm. She indicated with her head. Across the yard, leaning on the side of the Little Theater, Jack and Rachael were seeing exactly how far they could stick their tongues down each other's throats. At least that's what it looked like. To make it worse, Rachael was groping Jack's butt.

"Damn," she said. "Look at them!"

"Yeah. Gross, huh?"

"Are they always like that?"

"Pretty much. Why? Does it bother you?"

"No." She paused. "Well, yeah, kinda."

"Jules . . . ," I warned.

"It pisses me off."

I looked at her in amazement and started to smile. A very strange expression came across her face.

"What's going on, woman?" I asked.

"Nothing." She was obviously lying. "How do I look?"

"Good."

"Truth?"

"Truth."

"Okay, then, here I go."

Not knowing what Jules had in mind, I followed her down the rest of the stairs and walked with her across the yard. She went straight up to the twosome and stood there. Just stood there, waiting. Other people walked by, taking in the scene, and a few — who remembered the Jules/Jack relationship — stopped to see what she was up to. No one spoke, and so there was quite a crowd by the time Jack came up for air. He and Rachael literally jumped apart.

"Hi," Jules said.

"Oh . . . hi. I didn't see you," Jack answered, confused by the crowd. "What's going on?"

"Oh, not too much. I just finished doing almost seven months of chemotherapy, and I wanted to thank you for all the great phone calls and letters and stuff." She flashed a big Juliana smile. "They really meant a lot to me."

"What?" Jack was really confused now. "Uh, I didn't . . . um, write you or call or anything."

She let that sink in a minute. "No, you didn't, did you."

With that, she turned and walked away. I followed a few steps behind, catching up halfway across the yard. Jules was almost glowing.

"Girlfriend, you are amazing," I told her. "Where did that come from?" She shrugged.

Brooke and Colleen and Thea had seen the whole thing and rushed up, laughing. We all looked back. Rachael had flounced away, and Jack was left there alone, with his face hanging out. The people around him didn't know how to respond. Somebody started giggling. Somebody else told him to close his mouth.

"Maybe that wasn't such a good idea," Jules said. "Look at him."

"What?" Brooke jumped in. "Are you crazy?" She looked at Colleen. "I think she's crazy."

"Come on," Thea added. "We're getting you out of here."

"No, really," Jules said to them. "Now I feel bad."

"Get her arm," Colleen said to Thea, taking the other one. "Come on, Julie. Before you do something really stupid."

"But —," Julie protested feebly, smiling as she did.

"No, no, no," Brooke told her. "You are coming with us."

"But I have to meet my mom."

"Fine," said Brooke. "We'll take you."

I stood back, waiting for her to notice I wasn't with them. She didn't.

Later that night, Jack called me.

"I really don't appreciate what Julie did to me today," he started the conversation.

"So why are you telling me?"

"Because you're her best friend. You could talk to her."

"Jack, as much as I don't like you — and I don't — I think you ought to talk to Jules yourself. Calling me isn't going to solve anything."

"There's nothing to solve. She was totally out of line. I think she should apologize, to me *and* Rachael."

"Are you the densest person alive, or do you just like people to think so?"

"Don't start, okay?"

"I thought you were Julie's friend."

"Well, I thought so, too, until today."

"Then what's your problem? She has cancer, you shithead. She's been doing chemotherapy since July."

"I know that."

"Well, then, you should have called her, or written a letter, or sent a stupid card. How hard is that?"

"Well, she didn't call me, either."

I let that one sit there for a minute, in silence. I was beginning to doubt the boy's basic intelligence.

"Well, are you going to talk to her for me or what?"

"Talk to her yourself."

"Maybe I will. Thanks for nothing." He hung up.

I debated a minute, then called Jules. She answered on the second ring.

"Guess what?" I asked her.

"Where did you go?" she asked me.

"What?"

"This afternoon. Where'd you go?"

"What do you mean, where did I go? *You* left *me*."

"Well, why didn't you come with us?"

"Why didn't you ask me to?"

"Sam!"

"What?"

"Never mind. Nothing." She sighed, and there was a moment of silence.

"Anyway, I got a call from Jack," I said, and told her about our conversation.

"Whoa. Do you think he's gonna call me?" she asked.

"He might."

"Do you think I should apologize?"

"No! You didn't do anything wrong."

"Well, maybe not, but —"

"Shh! Are you coming back to Company this weekend?"

"As a matter of fact, I've been trying on my leotards," she told me. "I sure am skinny."

"Oh, yeah?"

"Well, anorexic is a better description. Hey, why don't you spend the night Friday? We could —"

"Sorry, I can't. I have plans with Paul."

"Oh." Her voice changed.

"You could go with us. We're just gonna see a movie."

"No, that's okay."

"Come on, Jules — I really want you to meet him. I told him all about you."

"Great. Look, I better go. Do you think you could still take me to dance? I'm not supposed to drive yet."

Paul and I had a great time seeing a movie Friday night, and I made sure to get home early so I'd be ready for Saturday. I picked Jules up at nine-fifteen, and we got to the studio even before Linda. We sat in the car and waited. Jules was quiet, and I wondered if she was mad about the night before. We had hardly talked at all on the drive there. Finally, watching her fuss with her wig and shoes and stuff, I realized she was nervous. She hadn't danced for months, and it was going to be hard for her to get back into it.

She looked at me a little sheepishly and spoke. "I don't think I ever understood how important it is for me to dance until I couldn't. It's such a gift."

"Yeah."

"Really. You leave here, and you go to this whole other reality. Just the dancer and the dance and the music. . . . Do you know what I mean?"

I started singing Cassie's song from *A Chorus Line:* "All I ever needed was the music . . . and the mirror . . . and the chance. . . ." I caught Jules's expression and stopped.

"Do you?" she asked, and stared at me with those chocolate eyes. She wasn't challenging — she was questioning, and I swallowed my smart-ass answer.

"I think I do."

"I'm glad."

We sat in silence for a few minutes. I was shy with her suddenly; the same kind of alienation and difference I'd felt before Christmas was there again. She was Jules, she was my One and Only, but she was forever altered by what she'd been through. I might share some of it with her, but there was no way I could share it all.

"Come on," she said, opening the car door. "There's Linda."

Linda was surprised and completely delighted to see Jules. They hugged and hugged, and I felt like I had suddenly disappeared.

"Thank you for all the letters," Jules told her as we went toward the studio door. "I really appreciated them."

"It was my pleasure," Linda said.

I looked at Jules. She had never said a thing about any letters from Linda.

"They were very important to me. Knowing someone else cared was . . . well, it helped a lot," Jules continued.

"Well, good, and I'm glad you're back. Can you dance?"

"I guess we'll find out. I sure want to."

The other girls started arriving, and Brooke and Colleen and Thea surrounded Jules again. I felt a bad mood descending. What was the big deal, anyway? If they had missed her so much, why hadn't they visited and spent time with her when she was sick? And why was she so pleased to see a bunch of people she used to say she didn't even really like? I knew I was being shitty and I couldn't seem to help myself. I went to the barre and started my pliés.

A few minutes later, Jules stood behind me. I glanced at her in the mirror. She was thinner than I had realized, fragile-looking and helpless. She started her pliés and I heard a big sigh.

"Are you okay?" I whispered.

"Yeah, but I'm really weak," she whispered back.

"Don't overdo it your first time back."

She nodded, and we continued to warm up. Midway through *tendues,* I whispered to her again. "Everybody's sure glad to see you."

"Yeah."

"It must make you feel really good."

"Yeah, it does," she said.

"Hey, after rehearsal, maybe you and I could —"

"Sam, I'm sorry, but I really need to concentrate."

"I know. I just thought —"

"*Dancers!*" Linda called out to us. "*No* talking."

Julie

After ending chemo and before I got back to my life, I rested for two weeks, then spent eight days at the Jerestin Cancer Institute near Santa Fe, New Mexico, to start a holistic course of treatment. I knew it would help. Dr. Harold Jerestin had come highly recommended, through the huge, unofficial, nationwide network of cancer patients who were all looking for the same solution. Several people raved about his program. My dad researched carefully and spent hours talking to Dr. Jerestin on the phone.

"The body is equipped to fight anything that attacks it, including cancer, *if* it is given the right tools," the doctor explained. "Your daughter needs a healthy macrobiotic diet, a strong emotional support system, and a positive, holistic attitude. I will determine the diet, provide a vitamin/mineral combination designed specifically for her, and counsel the family about attitude and support. You take the responsibility for getting her here, and pay the Institute whatever you can comfortably afford."

My dad stayed home with Rosie, and my mom and I went alone. We lived a week in a funky little motel near the clinic, in a room with severely awful puke green wallpaper and lumpy beds, but it didn't matter. We spent almost all of our time at the Institute.

The first day, we presented ourselves at nine, without a clue of what to expect. A uniformed male nurse led us down a long, comfortable hallway to a room that looked like someone's living room. We waited barely a moment before the door opened and then we looked at each other with surprise. Dr. Jerestin was incredibly good-looking, a Hollywood producer's idea of a genius doctor — disheveled, compelling, and intense. He wore blue jeans and a blue madras shirt, with a white doctor's jacket open over it and a stethoscope hanging around his neck. His eyes reminded me of Sam.

"Let's begin," he said, and gestured for us to sit on the couch. Looking directly at me, he continued. "First, tell me about your dancing."

I talked for almost two and a half hours, with his gentle questions leading me through dance, Jack, Sam, my parents, the chemo . . . everything. He listened intently to every single word. Finally, when I was done, he smiled.

"I think I can help you. Your mind-body connections are very well developed. You have a strong spiritual foundation — whether you know it or not. And the way you fought the chemotherapy shows incredible will. I think you're a survivor, and I'd like us to get to work."

I felt more enthusiastic than I had in months! We spent the rest of the week implementing the diet: no sugar, meat, fats, or processed foods; lots of veggies and whole grain rice and bread. He devised my own personal combination of vitamin horse pills. My mom and I learned meditation and how to focus on killing cancer cells and getting me well. I started to enjoy every moment of being awake.

I didn't mind the diet, even though the pills were big enough to choke an elephant. My mom and I laughed a lot, and the easiest thing in the world was keeping my attitude good.

We arrived home to a letter from the school board. "After careful consideration" of my "special circumstances," they had changed their collective mind. If I could manage to attend my English class for the rest of the year, they would let me "walk through" graduation with everyone else. I wouldn't actually get a diploma until all course requirements were satisfied, but who cared?

I went to school two days after we returned and I started Company that weekend. Never before had my dancing been so important. Everything was harder, and some things I just couldn't do, but I was there. My turns were off, my control had vanished, and we won't even talk about strength. But I was moving, and the music was talking to me, and it didn't hurt. Well, not all that much.

After my first rehearsal, I asked Linda if I had a chance of dancing in our big concert, since my parents would never let me go on the tour. She was thoughtful and looked at me carefully as she answered.

"You're pretty weak."

"I know, but I'll work hard."

"Is it all right with your doctor and your parents?"

"They don't make the decision," I told her, more defiantly than I intended. "*I* do." It wasn't entirely true.

She smiled. "If you dance in my show, you have to go all out. No excuses."

"I can do it." I hoped I could.

"I think you can, too. All right, then. You're in. But I'm not sure which numbers, okay?"

"Okay." I didn't have the energy to show it, but I was totally excited.

"It won't be 'The Blues Suite.' Or any of the new dances," she warned. "Even if you were strong, there wouldn't be time to rehearse them properly."

"That's fine. Really." And it was.

Linda was not the kind of person who would tell me something just to make me feel good. If *she* thought I could get it together enough to dance — well, somehow I would. It was February. The concert was at the end of April. I'd work slowly and steadily and get my stamina to the point where I could handle the choreography. It didn't matter which dances. Whatever she gave me, I'd do my absolute best.

I could hardly believe it. Everything was finally getting back to normal.

Sam

After New Year's, Paul and I started hanging out more and more. San Francisco's just a few minutes from Mill Valley if you have a car, so it was easy to see each other during the week sometimes, as well as on the weekends. Nothing seemed to bother me when we were together. We saw lots of movies and went on silly excursions. It seemed like we were always laughing. I thought maybe I was falling in love with him. I kinda wished I could talk it over with Jules, but even when we did manage some time together, she religiously avoided the subject.

Jules and I didn't carpool anymore. She was able to drive herself to school most of the time, and there was always Brooke, Colleen, Sarah, or Thea to pick her up. All of a sudden, she had tons of best friends. I noticed we hardly danced together at rehearsal, and even when I'd call her, she'd rarely call me back. Maybe it was the aftereffects of the chemo. Or maybe she was too caught up with all the attention she was getting from everybody. I didn't much like it, but I didn't say anything.

One Thursday, after she'd been back at school for a couple of weeks, we found ourselves walking out to the parking lot together at noon. She was heading for her car, to go home. I was going to meet Paul and go to lunch. I fell in beside her and slowed my pace to match hers.

"Hi."

"Hi, Sam."

"All done for the day?"

"Yeah. You, too?"

"No, I have to be back for seventh."

Just then, Paul pulled up beside us and rolled down his window.

"Am I late?"

"No, just right. Look who's here," I told him as I leaned in and gave him a little kiss. Jules kept walking toward her car.

"Jules!" I yelled. "Wait up. I want you to meet Paul."

She turned back with a weird little smile. Paul parked and got out.

"I'm glad to finally meet you, Jules," Paul said.

"Me, too," she replied. "But my name is *Julie.*"

"Sure, okay. Julie." He smiled his enormous smile and held out his hand. "I'm still glad to meet you." She took his hand, barely, and shook it.

"Well, I better go," she said. "See ya."

Paul took me to The Depot for lunch and then dropped me back at school. He didn't mention Jules at all, which I thought was kind. After my class, I went over to her house. She was in the backyard, reading.

"What's going on with you?" I asked.

"What do you mean?"

"I mean, did I do something to you? Are you mad at me?"

"No."

"Then why were you so rude to Paul?"

"What are you talking about?"

"You were rude. 'But my name is Julie'? What kinda shit is that?"

"Sam, you're making something out of nothing."

"I don't think so. I think you're really being an asshole."

"*Me?*" She put her book down and sat up really straight.

"Yeah. You never call me back. You never have time to talk to me at school. And now you're being rude to my boyfriend."

"*I* don't have time? What about you?"

"Me?"

"All you have time for is Paul."

"That's not true."

"It is so."

"It is not!"

"And when we *are* together, it's 'Paul this' and 'Paul that.' You barely even noticed I was back."

"Jules . . . you are *so* off. . . ."

"You didn't even call on Valentine's Day."

"You didn't call me, either. Listen —"

"I mean, it's okay," she interrupted. "I understand. But don't blame everything on me, all right? Look at yourself once in a while. You can be an asshole, too."

We glared at each other. Then she picked up her book, opened it, leaned back in the chair, and started reading. I didn't say anything else. I got up, walked out along the side of the house, and went home.

Paul called me that night around seven, to tell me he was on his way over. I almost didn't answer the phone. I kinda just wanted to sit and try to figure out why Jules was being such a jerk. He must've heard something in my voice.

"Whoa . . . you're bummed. What'd I do?" he asked.

"Nothing."

"Oh — your mom's home, huh?"

"No."

"Well, what's going on? You sound like death."

"Nothing, okay? Are you leaving now?"

"Maybe I better stay home. I wouldn't want to interrupt your bad mood."

"I'm not in a bad mood."

"Sure sounds like it."

"Look, if you don't wanna come over, it's fine with me. I've got a lot of homework anyway."

"You know, that'd probably be best."

"Fine."

There was a brief silence.

"Well, I better get off," I said.

"Wait. Do we still have plans for Friday?" he asked.

"Are you sure you want to? I might be in a bad mood or something."

"Sammie, I didn't mean it like that."

"Whatever."

"I just think you need some time alone."

"Fine."

"Okay, good. I'll see you tomorrow around seven. How about Italian?"

"Great. Bye."

I hung up, and somehow managed not to throw the phone across the room. How dare he? I pushed "talk" and dialed his number. It rang once, and I hung up again. This time, I put the porta-phone gently back in its holder. Two strikes in one day were quite enough. I wasn't up for one more.

I pulled out my physics homework and stared at it for twenty minutes, then realized I hadn't eaten dinner. I fixed myself some cereal and raisins and went back to physics. I still couldn't concentrate enough to make sense of it. Finally I tossed the book to the floor. This was ridiculous. The two people I loved most in the world had just deserted me, and I couldn't think of a single thing to do about it.

The evening dragged on forever; then Friday raced by. At school, I saw Jules briefly but didn't get a chance to speak to her. After school, I had rehearsal for "The Blues Suite." We worked until almost six, so I barely finished showering before Paul was at my door. My mom let him in. I could hear them in the living room, laughing and talking, and all of a sudden I got nervous. I tried on four outfits before I settled on what I would wear to dinner.

On the way to the Blue Rock Inn in Larkspur, Paul acted like nothing had happened. I started to relax. As he drove, he talked about his day. I watched him and appreciated — again — how good-looking he was. During dinner, he kept me laughing with stories about his mom and dad's divorce.

"You're amazing," I told him as we sipped *caffè latte*s and shared a piece of chocolate pie.

"Of course I am." He toasted me with his cup.

"No, I mean it. When my parents got divorced, I was crazed. You just laugh about it."

"What's the choice? It's stupid to be depressed all the time."

"I wasn't exactly depressed."

"No?"

"No. I was pissed off and, I don't know, kinda lost.

Definitely screwed up. If it hadn't been for Jules, I don't know what I would've done."

"You would have been fine."

"You don't know that."

"Yeah, you would have."

I took a bite of pie and considered what he'd said. "You don't like Jules much, do you?"

"I don't know her."

"Is it because she was rude when you guys met?"

"Sammie, let's not talk about her, huh?"

"Why not?"

"Because you always get upset."

"I do not."

"Yes. You do."

"I just want to know what you thought of her."

"Why?"

"I don't know. Because I do."

"Okay. She was . . . fine. Great. I don't know what you want me to say."

"Don't you think she's pretty?"

"Sammie . . ."

"Come on," I teased. "That's not hard."

Paul looked away from me and had a hard time looking back. He shifted in his seat, took a sip of his *latte,* and finally found my eyes. "You're not going to like this."

I didn't say anything.

"Julie may have been a pretty girl before she got sick. But the person I met was just . . . scary-looking. I don't understand how you can be around her."

"She's my best friend."

"Maybe, but she's bad news, Sammie."

"What do you mean?"

"I mean . . . it's obvious. Because she's . . . you know."

"No, I don't."

"Well, if I were you, I'd just end the friendship now. It'd be easier on you. That's all."

All of a sudden I was looking at a person I'd never seen before. "Maybe you should take me home."

"See, I told you. We talk about Julie and you get all upset."

"I'm not upset."

"Not much." He looked around, caught the waiter's eye, and motioned for the check. Then he focused back on me. "I guess I just have a different philosophy about things."

"I guess you do."

"Sammie, believe me. You've got to take care of yourself first. You shouldn't stress out like this."

"I'd really like to go."

"Sure." He paid the check, and we walked out to his car, neither of us saying another word.

Julie

I couldn't sleep at all Thursday night, and not just because of the fight with Sam. My leg and hip were hurting again, bad. I figured it was from all the dancing I'd been doing. Linda was working with me two afternoons a week, and the company's rehearsals were going four hours every Saturday. Obviously I hadn't fully recovered my strength.

As I was settling into bed, the old searing pain shot through me. I had to bite my lip to keep from yelling for my mom. She'd overreact and call doctors, when all I really needed was to relax and to sleep. I took a painkiller and propped my leg up with extra pillows. The pain finally started to slip away, but my mind refused to quit. Over and over, it played back the afternoon — meeting Paul and, just hours later, calling my best friend an asshole.

She was right. I had been rude to him. But it wasn't on purpose. I was simply tired of being put on display. The cancer had made me a kind of celebrity at school, and suddenly I had plenty of "friends." And every time I went there, I'd watch them pretend I looked normal. I'd walk by groups of people that would suddenly get silent and smile too much. By the end of the morning, I'd be drained.

I'd need to be away from eyes and faces. I thought Sam would realize all that. But there she'd been, showing me off like everybody else. She'd shoved Paul in my face, and I'd gone through it all again. He'd been disgusted. So I'd been rude. And she'd gotten mad.

I guess I had expected Sam to be able to see things from my point of view. She used to understand everything. But then, things used to be easier to understand.

By morning, the pain in my leg had escalated. I thought briefly about calling Sam for a ride, but I wasn't up to the encounter. I took the two last painkillers and decided to give myself another day before reporting to my mom or calling Dr. Jerestin. I was overwhelmingly tired. No doubt that made the pain seem worse than it really was. Briefly I considered staying home, but then I would have to deal with my mom.

I went to class, and knew it was the right place to be. The pills had taken the edge off the pain and removed me somewhat from the people. We were having a study hall, to prepare for a big test I wasn't expected to take, so I kicked back on the red beanbag chair Mr. Gilmore had brought in for me and closed my eyes. And listened. Over to my left, Mr. Gilmore and a group of girls were discussing *Crime and Punishment.* A boy and a girl behind me were drilling each other on vocabulary words. I could hear a soft, raspy snore — someone was sleeping. I smiled to myself. Everything was so wonderfully boring.

The pain came back an hour later, pretty strong, just as I was leaving class. I stopped at the top of the staircase to catch my breath and be sure my leg would support me. From behind came a voice I didn't recognize.

"Hey, Julie, you okay?" I turned to look. It was Ralph, a big, shy, football player I hardly ever talked to.

"Yeah," I told him, trying to smile. "My leg hurts a little. That's all."

"How 'bout a ride, then?" he asked, and before I could reply, he scooped me up in his arms and bounded down the stairs. People smiled at us and got out of the way.

"Where's your car?" he demanded when we reached the bottom, still holding me gently.

"Back lot, but you don't have to —"

He started through the yard. People kept smiling. Thea called out, "Way to go, Julie!" I saw Sam standing by the science building, but Ralph whisked me right by and I barely had a chance to wave. He carried me all the way to my car and deposited me with a little nod by the door. Before I could thank him, he turned and was gone. I smiled at his back.

Halfway home, the pain attacked. I pulled up to my house and was relieved to see my mom's car gone. I didn't want to tell her about my leg quite yet. I parked the car and went inside, trying not to limp. I found some nonprescription painkillers and figured I could safely take four. I was in the kitchen, halfway through with my glass of water, when my dad came around the corner. We both jumped.

"Shit, Daddy!" I said as I dropped the water glass. "You scared me."

"Sorry." He didn't mention my cussing.

"Hey, why are you here? Are you sick or something?"

"No, I had to take my car in." He shrugged. "It seemed a good excuse for a day off."

"Oh. Good. Where's Mom?"

"Some lunch thing at Rosie's school." He glanced at the pill bottle in my hand but didn't say anything. Then he grabbed the dustpan and brush from the closet and bent over to clean up the glass.

We found ourselves hanging out together in the living room, and he clicked on the television. He tried several channels. Then he clicked it off.

"I don't know why we even have this thing," he complained. "There's never anything good on anymore."

"Well, Rosie likes it."

"Rosie watches it entirely too much."

He was right of course, but I wondered if some of that came from not having her mom and dad around. Mom had spent most of the last year taking care of me, and even though Daddy was around, he managed to stay distant.

"Daddy, do you think Rosie's going to be all right?" The question came out of nowhere, and we were both a little surprised.

"I'm afraid I don't understand what you're asking."

"I mean, with me and everything."

He shook his head. "I still don't understand."

He obviously didn't want to talk about it, but something pushed me on. "Well, how much do you think she understands about what's happening? With the cancer?"

He started looking around for a magazine or paper to read. "I really don't know." He found the morning comics and opened them up.

"It must be so weird for her. Especially during the chemo."

"I suppose."

"Hey, remember how she used to yell at me when I was doing a show?" I smiled.

"Hmm?"

"You know. The second I'd come on stage, she'd start screaming, 'There's Julsie, there's my Julsie! That's my sister!' I hated it."

"Did you?" He wasn't really listening.

"Well, it was embarrassing. Everybody would start laughing. But I guess it was cute. Mom said she did it 'cause she loves me." I sighed, thinking how awful I'd been to her lately. "I wonder what she thinks about me now."

"Oh, I'm sure she still loves you."

"I don't know. I keep planning how I'll explain it to her someday. When she's older and I'm better."

"That'll be nice."

"Yeah, it will." I stared at him as he continued to read the comics. All of a sudden there was so much I wanted to ask him. "Daddy, do you ever wonder —"

"You know," he interrupted, "I ought to take advantage of this time and get that lawn mowed."

That night I went to sleep early. The tiredness was worse, the pain was throbbing, and I felt achy and horrible. I told my mom I needed to save up strength for the weekend rehearsals and managed to get into bed without her asking a thousand questions. The phone rang about eleven. I let the answering machine pick up and listened. It was Sam.

"Are you there? If you're there, please pick up. . . . Okay, look, what do you say we go to dinner tomorrow night? Huh? To Joe's? They've got healthy stuff. You can eat plain lettuce or something." There was a pause, and the machine clicked off. Sam called back and continued, "You're right. I was an asshole. I'm sorry. I miss you. *Please* call me if you get this before midnight. Okay? Otherwise I'll see you at rehearsal. I love you."

I smiled but didn't call back. My leg was getting steadily worse, and I wouldn't be able to concentrate on a conversation. I thought about yelling for my mom, but what could she do? I focused on my breathing, and eventually I slept.

The next thing I knew, my mom's voice woke me up. "Julie . . . Julie, wake up."

I opened my eyes, closed them again, and turned over on my side, away from her.

"Go away, please."

"Honey, it's almost nine o'clock. You have rehearsal at ten."

"Okay, okay. Just one more minute."

"Good girl. I'll start your breakfast."

Ten minutes later she came back. I had fallen asleep again.

"Julie, turn over, honey," she said. She put her hand on my forehead. "Sweetie, you're burning up. I'm going to get the thermometer." My temperature was almost 104. "I'm calling the doctor," she told me.

"Not Dr. Conner?"

"No, just a regular doctor." She called Campton Medical and arranged an appointment for early that afternoon.

"So I can go to dance first?" I asked hopefully.

"Not a chance, kid."

"But Mom . . ."

"Shhh . . . go back to sleep. Linda will understand."

Doctors at Campton Medical consult one another when they're not sure of something, so, again, I ended up seeing several. One doctor said it was probably a virus. Another said it could be a bacterial infection. Antibiotics were prescribed and they all agreed I should rest.

By Monday, my fever had gone away, but I still had no energy and no will to be out of bed. My very bones were tired. It was a chore to get up to go to the bathroom. I couldn't manage English class, and my mom arranged for assignments to be sent home. Then she called Linda and canceled the entire week's rehearsals. I raged at her.

"Linda says not to worry," she explained calmly. "The concert's not till the end of April. This is only the first week of March. She thinks you'll be just fine."

Sam and Thea and Colleen each called a couple of times. I started feeling guilty about not calling back and changed my answering machine message to say, "I love you all, but I won't be getting back to you for a while."

At the end of the week, my mom called Dr. Conner. We set up an appointment for the same afternoon.

"You look awful" were the first words out of the good doctor's mouth.

I didn't respond. She was right.

"Well, come on in," she said. "Let's take a good look at you."

We went into the examining room. I climbed on the table and let her look into my eyes and mouth and ears. She took my blood pressure and drew blood for tests. Then she had me lie down on my back, and she moved my legs around, watching my face as she did.

"Hurts, huh?" she asked.

"Not really."

"Liar."

My mom started to open her mouth to defend me. I interrupted before she began.

"It hurts," I admitted.

"Like before. Right?"

"Right."

She looked at me and then up at my mom. She had absolutely no expression on her face.

"Let's do another CAT scan. And see what the blood count says."

My heart started pounding. I was back to Square One, only this time I knew what all the procedures were. I wasn't scared of them like the first time around. But I *was* scared.

It was hours before we finished everything. I was exhausted and leaning on my mom as we waited in Dr. Conner's office for her to come back with "the results." It didn't take her long.

She didn't simply open the door and come in; she injected herself into the space. Her expression now was quite clear — she was mad. I felt my mom pull herself up and get ready to fight if it was necessary. It wasn't. Dr. Conner's anger wasn't aimed directly at us.

"I'm not quite sure where to start," she informed us, warning with her tone that we had better get ready to listen. "Perhaps by asking you the specifics of the so-called treatment you say you've been taking?"

"Well," I began, "I, uh —"

"It isn't a 'treatment,' Dr. Conner," my mom helped out. "It's an approach to helping the body heal itself. Julie has a good healthy diet and does imaging to —"

"Julie's 'good healthy diet,' " Dr. Conner interrupted, "has made her anemic. Dangerously so. That's one of the reasons you're feeling tired. I'm surprised, after reading the blood workup, that you walked in here on your own steam. You don't have any white cells to speak of. If you caught a cold right now, it would probably kill you." My mom started to reply, but Dr. Conner held up her hand, then continued to speak.

"The CAT scan shows three brand-new areas of growth. The original areas have increased in size. Regardless of what you think is happening with your 'approach,' the reality is, the cancer is stronger than ever."

My mother stood up. "Julie's going to wait outside for a few minutes," she announced, then looked at me. "If that's okay with you, sweetie?" I shrugged. She took my arm and escorted me to the outer office. I sat on the chair in the corner, not sure what I was feeling or thinking. I knew I should assert myself, demand to hear whatever Dr. Conner might say, but the words wouldn't come. I was too damn tired. My mom kissed me on the forehead.

"I'll just be a few minutes. If you need anything, give a holler." I nodded and started trying to get comfortable. It wasn't easy. My mom went back in and shut the door quietly behind her.

I could hear her talking, quietly but intensely. The words weren't there, but the tone was clear. Dr. Conner answered, her tones as angry as they had been a moment before. Most of me was happy to stay exactly where I was. It was hard to care what they were saying, and I hurt — lots. But a small, stubborn part of me made me move closer to the door. I wasn't sure I wanted any more facts than I already had, but neither did I want to go back to letting someone else control my life. So there I was. By sitting in a chair nearby and leaning into the door, I could hear almost everything.

". . . and if you had continued the chemotherapy as I suggested," Dr. Conner was proclaiming, "we may not have had the further incidence. We may have been able to contain the cells. I don't think you people understand the consequences of making such a foolish decision —"

"I understand," my mom interrupted, "but I'm not sure we're talking about the same thing. My primary concern is Juliana. All of her. That means how she feels emotionally as well as spiritually as well as physically."

"That's very noble of you."

There was a definite pause before my mother continued.

"Dr. Conner, I resent your tone and your attitude. It would be helpful to think that your interest in Julie went beyond some little scoreboard you must keep in your desk somewhere. Cancer, one; Dr. Conner, zero."

"If my attitude offends you, I would be happy to recommend another oncologist. I don't feel there are any here as qualified as I, but it is certainly your choice."

My mom paused again.

"Dr. Conner, do you have children?"

"No, but I don't see what that —"

"Maybe that's what's missing. Please don't misunderstand — I'm not criticizing your professional ability. I know you've done everything in your power to help Julie. I only wish you could find some way to take the whole person into account when you talk to her or when you treat her. She's seventeen years old. You don't have to speak so bluntly to a child."

It was quiet for a second, and when she spoke again, Dr. Conner's voice sounded low and hurt and tired.

"Mrs. Michaels, I've been treating children with cancer for over twenty years. There is no nice way to talk about it. I don't mean to hurt Julie's feelings. I don't mean to scare her. But she is terminal, and, regardless of her age,

I feel she's entitled to know exactly what is going on."

There was a silence so long I thought maybe I should go back to my seat. Then my mom's voice, low and stern.

"You're not to say a word."

"Excuse me?"

"I don't want Juliana to know what you've just told me."

"Now, Mrs. Michaels, I —"

"You may talk to Julie about possible treatments and their effects. You may certainly tell her any advantages you might see to reinstating chemo, which I am assuming is what you want to do."

"That's correct."

"You will not mention anything else."

"Mrs. Michaels, I —"

"She's my daughter, Dr. Conner. She is seventeen years old. If what you say is true, there is nothing to be done. But I will not have her burdened by your need to be explicit."

"I understand."

"Good, I hope you do. It will be her decision, then, whether to go back to chemo. Have I been clear?"

"Completely."

Then nothingness. Outside me, everything had stopped. Inside, my heart and my ears and my throat and my head were pounding in rhythm. I had stopped breathing, had to tell myself to take a breath. The whole of me — my skin, my fingers, my face, my arms and legs — all tingled, then turned hot. Somehow I had the presence of mind to walk back to my original chair. I sat down just as my mom opened the office door and even managed to look up and smile as she came out.

Sam

After dinner that Friday, Paul and I drove home without talking. There didn't seem to be anything else to say. He pulled up to my house and leaned over and gave me a kiss. Then I got out and he drove off and I went inside. My mother, of course, was out. I plopped onto the couch and held my head in my hands. I didn't want to think or talk or move.

Ten minutes later, Paul knocked on the door.

"I think we need to talk," he said when I opened the door.

My stomach dropped. "Sure. Come on in." We sat at opposite ends of the couch.

"I'm not sure where to start," he said.

I waited without speaking. He shifted around and then focused his gaze on me.

"I really like you, Sammie. I think I could even be in love with you. I mean, you're *so* pretty. And you're funny and we really have a good time together, but . . ." He stopped.

"But . . . what?"

"Well, I just think we should take a break from each other for a while. You know what I mean?"

I didn't answer.

He continued. "Maybe just for a few weeks — I don't know. Maybe a month. Just to have a chance to think about things, you know?"

"Is this because of Julie?"

"No, not at all."

"Then I don't understand."

He shrugged and stood up. I stood up, too.

"Look, I just need some time away. That's all. It won't be forever." He started moving toward the door. "I'll call you in a few weeks and we can get together, and then we'll see. Okay?"

All of a sudden, I felt like I was talking to my father.

"Fine. I'll see you then." I opened the door.

"I knew you'd understand." He smiled and hugged me and escaped.

I didn't cry. I didn't get mad. I didn't feel anything, really. I stared at my bedroom walls for about an hour, and then I picked up the phone and called Jules. I didn't know what I was going to say, and when her machine answered, I apologized. Then I hung up and started to cry. I couldn't tell exactly why — if it was Jules or Paul or a combination of both. I just felt so incredibly alone.

Jules missed rehearsal the following day. Then she missed the whole week of school. I called twice more, until she changed her message. When she didn't show up to dance the following Saturday, I asked Linda if she'd heard anything. She nodded.

"I talked to Sandra. Julie is anemic, from the diet she's been on," Linda explained. "It may take a few weeks for her to be strong enough to come back to dance. Haven't you talked to her?"

I shook my head and shrugged a little. "I called, but she never called me back."

"Well, don't worry. She's okay. Knowing Julie, she'll be dancing again before we know it. Now, you get to work."

Thinking about calling is not the same as actually doing it. There was a time I wouldn't have even bothered thinking. I would have called, too bad if she didn't want to hear from me, and gone over if she hadn't called me back. This time I just thought about it. And thought about it. And thought about it. A little less each day, actually. The second week she was out, people started asking me where she was, and the rumors began, all kinds of stupid things. I made it a point to tell everybody she knew what Linda had said. "Anemic" wasn't very interesting, so they stopped worrying. Pretty soon I stopped worrying, too.

Or maybe I didn't actually stop. More like I put Jules in a drawer in the back of my mind, the one right next to Paul, and my father, and probably everything else that was bothering me. She wasn't any less important; she just wasn't immediate. Other things were happening. School was hard, people were finding out what colleges they could go to, and everyone was making plans for summer. Rehearsals for the concert were getting intense. And now that Paul and I weren't together, I was hanging around a lot with Brooke and her friends. She kept us on a pretty awesome social schedule.

"Wanna come to a luau?" she asked me the next Saturday during rehearsal. "It's tonight, nine until whenever. At Stinson, at Ginny-somebody's house."

"Sure," I answered. I couldn't think why not.

✿ ✿ ✿

A lot of Company kids were going, so we went as a group. The party was huge — it spilled out of three or four houses and all over the beach. I danced, laughed, flirted, and had the best time. Around two in the morning, I found myself at Mim's, a twenty-four-hour coffeehouse, with Colleen, Sarah, Thea, and Brooke. We giggled and talked and speculated about the people we'd seen at the party.

"I took numbers," Brooke announced, munching on an onion ring.

"You did what?" Thea asked, giggling.

"I took phone numbers. Anybody who wanted mine — I got theirs instead. And I asked them to write a description of themselves on the back." She shoved her hand into her jacket pockets and came out with a dozen or more little slips of paper. She proudly dropped them in the center of the table. We burst into laughter.

"You're so random," Sarah said. "Look, check it out"— and she picked up one of the papers. " 'Intense blue eyes, not tall, but definitely built.' Oh, man."

" 'Great bod — BIG HANDS' is my favorite," Colleen said. "You know what they say about the size of a guy's hands, doncha?"

"You gonna call any of them?" Sarah asked when we finally got ourselves under control.

"Are you kidding? I can't even remember which is what."

"Oh, come on — let's call Big Hands!" Thea urged.

"No way," Brooke said.

"I'll do it," I said.

"You would not," Brooke countered.

"I would so. Give it here." I took the paper, and we all

went in the back where the pay phones were. As I dialed, the giggling got intense. The phone started ringing and I shushed them with a gesture. Then a deep male voice came on the line. I held the receiver so they all could listen.

"Your dime . . . ," he said. Sarah rolled her eyes.

"Hi . . . ," I said in my lowest, sexiest tone, "is this Big Hands?" Thea fell on the floor, holding her mouth, giggling out of control.

"Uh, yeah. As a matter of fact."

"Well, my name is Brooke . . ." Brooke made a face and punched me. I moved away from her. ". . . and I'd really like to come to your house right now and see your big hands, if only I knew where you lived."

"Yeah, well, why not. Got a pencil?" Brooke grabbed the phone from me and hung it up. We erupted into laughter and somehow made our way back to the table. The people around us complained to the waitress, and she came over and asked us to stop. We couldn't, quite, but we lowered the volume a bit.

"I can't believe you did that," Colleen said, incredulous.

"I can't believe you used my name!" Brooke added.

"What would you have done if you got the address?" Thea asked.

"Gone over. What else?"

"You would not!" Brooke insisted.

"Oh, no? You don't know me very well," I insisted. "One time, Jules and I were at this —"

The silence was immediate. I stopped, too, feeling her absence, realizing that I hadn't been missing her at all. I hadn't even thought about her. A person I would never have gone to a party without, my One and Only. She was sitting at home, trying to get strong enough to go to school and to dance, and I had laughed a whole night without one thought. A lot of nights, in fact. I smiled, a little embarrassed. The girls were watching me with strange looks on their faces. I knew they were thinking about her now, too. The quiet got intense. We all picked at our food. Brooke picked up the phone numbers and began folding them in tiny squares.

"It's so weird," Colleen finally said in a strange little voice. "Julie, I mean."

"Yeah," Sarah said. "My mom says she's really sick again."

"My mom says there's no way she's going to make it," Brooke added.

"It's so unfair," said Sarah.

"She's anemic, guys — that's all," I told them. "No big deal."

Nobody answered. I reached for my purse and pulled out a few dollars. My hands were trembling. I tried smiling, but my face wouldn't do it. I could feel how stupid it looked, trying and not being able to fit into a smile. I stood up.

"Hey, I hafta go. Sorry — I didn't realize how late it was. Everybody have a ride home?"

They nodded, and I gathered up my stuff. They were all looking at me, and I didn't know what to feel.

"See you guys."

Outside, alone, it was fully fifteen minutes before I could stop my body from shaking enough so that I could start my car.

Julie

What happened to me in the following weeks happened to two people simultaneously. One of them, the Outside Me, listened carefully to Dr. Conner's arguments about going back to chemotherapy. She was quite literal about not saying what she agreed with my mom not to say. She explained that I had felt so good after chemo had stopped because the effects of the drugs were long-reaching. The cancer cells were still being kept from growing, and I wasn't having the poison put in my body. As soon as the effects wore off, though, the cancer cells started to grow again. That's why the pain had come back. As far as the alternative "treatment," it was hard for her not to go off completely. I could tell she thought it was stupid and useless. Given the anemia that had come from the "healthy diet," I had to agree with her. Old Dr. Jerestin hadn't helped a bit. She finished with her plea to continue a course of chemotherapy that would stop the spread of the cells. The Outside Me was quite mature. I asked questions.

"Will it be like before?"

"In some ways. You won't feel great right after."

"Will I sleep all the time?"

"Not if I change the dosage."

"Will I be able to continue dancing?"

"You'll have less pain in your hip. And if you have the strength to do it, I see no problem."

"What about this anemic stuff? I thought you couldn't do chemo with a low white count."

"You're right. We'll have to get you healthy again first."

"How?"

"Change your diet, mostly. Add some iron supplements. Blood will help. We can arrange a series of transfusions. It'll take a few weeks."

"I don't want blood from the blood bank."

"Julie, it's perfectly safe. There are tests —"

"Everyone says you can still get AIDS from it."

"All right. You can arrange for private donors. Anyone who has your blood type and is over eighteen."

"Okay, one last question."

"I'm all ears."

"Will I lose my hair again?"

She paused for a minute and looked at me, then shook her head, as if she couldn't believe what I had asked.

"Will I lose my hair again?" I repeated, not really caring what she thought.

"Not necessarily. I can adjust the dosage and alter the choice of drugs."

"But you can't be sure?"

Again, she gave me that look.

"Is it really that important to you?"

"Yes."

"Then I can be sure. You won't lose your hair."

"You promise?"

"I promise."

"Okay, then," I told her.

The Outside Me had decided to do it. The Inside Me

was still cowering from Dr. Conner's words to my mom. I could feel the separation happening. It was almost a physical sensation, a pulling apart. The Outside Me stepped forward and put on her armor. I could hear her asking and answering questions in the conversation with Dr. Conner, and I marveled at her competence, her utter cool in the face of this usually intimidating character. At the same time, the Inside Me shook and shivered, didn't know what to do or how to begin to do it. How to assimilate the information received in the past few hours. Where to put the proclamation of my death.

Strange how easy it was to become disassociated from myself. How very simple to slip into separate identities. The "I" of me, whatever that was, stood back and watched, evaluating what the Outside Me and the Inside Me were doing. But "I" didn't actually participate. "I" had become a nonentity, a nothing, a Not-Self. And yet no one would have realized what was going on. Outside Me was in charge of the entire masquerade, and she was doing herself proud.

After talking with Dr. Conner, I went in search of my mom. She had gone around the corner to the patients' lounge and was sitting by herself at the table, having a glass of Coke. She sipped at it, not paying much attention, and didn't see me come in. I stood by the doorway a moment to watch her. She looked different. Older, smaller, diminished somehow from "Mother." Mothers always know all. This person was lost. Did she have a Not-Self, too? I wondered. An Outside Mom and an Inside Mom? Maybe even a part that wasn't a mom, was instead just a woman wishing she didn't have to hang out at hospitals and get up five times in the middle of the night.

Suddenly I was angry at her. Big anger — very big. It

hit my head from the back and made my eyes water. My breathing got faster, and I could hear my heart pounding. Of course she could be calm. Of course she was in control. This wasn't happening to her; it was happening to me. I was going to be hooked up to poison again, not my mother. It was my solo journey. It didn't really involve her at all.

She should've been able to make it better. She should've been able to keep me from having to go through all this pain. But she didn't. She couldn't. She couldn't stop it, she couldn't change it, she couldn't fix a thing. What was wrong with her? She had always promised to keep me safe. How could she let me get cancer?

My mom looked up just then, and for less than an instant, not quite a heartbeat, there was a truth between us. Her eyes, mine; two bodies that had been one; two lives that were forever attached. Everything else was suspended. We stood in between time. But the feeling was too pure. It couldn't exist in the real world, this place of diseases and doctors. It disappeared, evaporated. We replaced it with smiles: hers a mom smile — reassuring, comforting, reaching out; mine in response only, no intent. I accepted what she was trying to give. Both of us knew it was a charade. Both of us agreed to play. What else could we do?

I joined her at the table. She slid her Coke over to me, and I sat down and took a sip. She smiled a question, tilting her head in a way she does when we both know what she's asking.

"I'm going to do it," Outside Me said with a small sense of confidence. "The chemo."

"All right." She nodded and kept smiling. "If you're sure

it's what you want. Dr. Conner hasn't influenced your decision?"

"No. She explained some stuff, and I made the choice. I think it'll be for the best. She says I won't lose my hair and I can keep on dancing." I smiled back at her. "What more could I want?"

My mom's face changed but didn't change. She was still smiling, but there was another layer there, underneath. I couldn't tell what it was, but it felt familiar. Almost like her Inside Self passing under her Outside One.

Sam

It wasn't until April that Jules came back to school. Then it wasn't for classes. She came in the late morning, with her mom. I caught a glimpse of them from across the yard. They were going up the stairs to the deans' offices. I followed them but was too late — they'd gone inside and shut the door. Waiting for ten minutes made me late to ethics class so I checked back afterward. They'd already left. I went back outside for lunch. Jack came up to me, without Rachael, for once.

"Hey — what's going on with Julie?" he asked.

" 'Hey'?"

"Hello, Samantha, how are you? Now, what's going on with Julie?"

"I keep telling you, if you want to know something about Jules, call her."

"What am I supposed to say — 'Why do you look so terrible?' "

A cold feeling went through my body. I hadn't seen Jules for over a month. Today I'd seen her only from a distance.

"What are you talking about?"

"She looks terrible — I don't know how else to put it.

I thought maybe you knew what was going on."

"She's anemic, stupid. Where have you been?"

"I don't think it's just that, Sammie."

"Leave me alone, okay? I'm trying to eat."

"You may not believe this, but I do care about Julie. I'm not trying to be an asshole. I just thought her best friend would know something. Sorry."

He shook his head at me and left. I saw him later, talking to Rachael and two other girls. They turned to stare at me. I had one class to go after lunch. I decided to cut it and went home.

What was going on with me? March had disappeared in a jumble of school, parties, evenings out with friends, and dance. Ever since that last night with Paul, I couldn't seem to get myself together. Everything was rushing by — I couldn't catch it. There didn't seem to be any time to think. Especially not about Jules. Three times I went to the phone. Twice I actually dialed her number. The first time the machine answered, and I hung up. The second time, Jules picked up.

"Hello?"

She sounded tired, and she sounded like she really didn't want to talk to anyone. I didn't speak.

"Hello . . . I can't hear you if you're there." She paused. "Okay, whoever you are, I'm hanging up now."

Sitting alone in my house, I could feel my face turning red. How stupid I was, how insensitive to her. Why couldn't I talk to her? What was the big deal? Then I remembered she hadn't called me, either. Not once in the past three and a half weeks. Whatever was going on was going on with both of us, and it would have to work itself out. It wasn't the first time we'd been mad at each other.

Except this time it wasn't exactly mad. We'd had a fight. But I'd apologized. So why was I feeling angry?

Nothing was making any sense. I took out books and tried to focus on my homework, but too many images were crowding my head. Jules and me out together, talking, laughing. Jules and me on her bed late at night, trying to figure out why life was like it was. Jules taking my arm and pulling me out of the house one day when my mom was screaming at me and throwing things. Jules crying in my arms. Me crying in hers. Then Jules in the hospital. Jules losing her hair. Jules and me at the beach, talking and talking, sitting and staring. Jules being pissy about meeting Paul. Me being jealous of her other friends. Too much had happened in the past year. I couldn't sort it out. I couldn't find her. And I couldn't find myself.

That Saturday, Jules came back to dance. She was there when I arrived, talking quietly with Linda in the corner. She saw me when I came in — I know she did — but she kept on talking. Several other girls were there already, and I could feel them watching. I put down my dance bag and took out my jazz shoes. I felt stuck and at the same time obligated to do something. I crossed over to them.

"Hi, Linda. Hi, Jules," I said, trying to keep my voice normal. My throat hurt. Jules looked down and slightly away from me.

"Could you give us just a minute, Sammie?" Linda asked.

"Sure."

I turned and walked over to the barre without knowing how I did it. My face felt hot, and all the anger from a few days before exploded inside. I started doing pliés, like a robot. Colleen joined me.

"Is she okay?" she asked.

It was good Linda started rehearsal before I had to answer, because I didn't know what to say. After the warmup, she went right into running our dances. Jules worked by herself toward the back. I decided to avoid looking at her in the mirror. It didn't matter. She was completely focused on herself.

When it was time for "The Little Girls' Dance," the duet everyone wanted to perform, Linda called out two pairs of names.

"Sarah and Colleen, I'll see you first. Then Sammie and Julie, you give it a try."

I couldn't believe it. We were back to the same two groups we'd originally had. How was I going to dance this with Jules? She didn't want to look at me, to have anything to do with me. That was obvious. Plus we hadn't rehearsed and hadn't actually danced together for over a month. I didn't watch Sarah and Colleen. They danced, and I was completely unaware. All of a sudden, everyone was clapping. Linda congratulated them and called for Jules and me.

We took our places, sitting, holding hands like little girls, frozen in a children's game. I was aware of Jules's hands, her long delicate fingers. And the touch of her. She was very cold. The music started: "Saturday Afternoon in '63," by Rikki Lee Jones. And with the cue, we started to move. Not just move — no, we started to dance. Together. We danced the little girls' games, and Jules mimed taking a ribbon from my hair, in play, and throwing it up to the sky. As I watched it come down, I turned to her smiling, innocent, and she was looking at me, knowing something I didn't yet understand. Our game continued, but now it was broken, and as we danced our growing up, growing apart, growing older, I couldn't tell where the music stopped and we began. The end came — years later, walking our separate ways, seeing each other, recognizing and reaching out, wanting to know if there still was a connection. We touched and, in the last moment, looked up. The imaginary ribbon was floating down again. Jules pointed to it, and on the final note, I reached up and grabbed it.

We held the picture. There was silence. No one moved; no one clapped. What was going on? We couldn't have been that bad. Then, out of nowhere, the applause. I looked at the group. Brooke was crying and Linda had tears in her eyes. I looked over at Jules, but she didn't seem to notice. She grabbed her dance bag and went out the door, just as Linda announced we'd be performing the dance.

Julie

Dance was more than a thing I did. It was my definition and my strength. It could reach out and bring me back to myself. It made me real and whole and strong. No one could take it or keep me from it. And no one, except maybe another dancer, could understand how it felt.

I remember dancing at the ocean one morning, years ago, when Rosie was still a baby and my family rented a cabin at Stinson Beach. It was not quite seven. No one was up; I left a note and planned to take a long walk, to see if I could make it all the way around the bluff at the northern end, but I never got that far. The ocean started talking to me, low and seductive — first a whisper, then an invitation, and finally, a promise. I went and sat close to the water, holding my knees to my chest and listening, listening. A calm came — a long, easy feeling that made me sigh big and let my shoulders go. Then a song. No words, no music of the kind humans make, but a song nevertheless, a rhythm and a melody and a meaning. Almost without my approval, a second before I was aware of it, my arms started to lift and my legs extended. The breath in my lungs was exhaled, and the next that I drew was in rhythm with the ocean.

I began a dance for my soul. It wanted no audience, no approval, no applause. It wanted only itself. It was me and the ocean and the movement and the song — one. Time was suspended. I had no world outside the moments; no needs, no cares, no reality except the dance. I danced until I came to the end, then stopped. For a moment after, I couldn't tell where I was, or why, but I knew myself and I understood how I was connected to the world.

And now. Now when I most needed my savior, I couldn't find it. Too much stood between. The connection was broken and tattered. Even the connections inside, the muscles to the bones, seemed incapable. The chemo helped with the pain but sapped my stamina. There was no reaching for that bit more; I could barely complete the warmup. The freedom of moving without pain, the confidence of a conditioned, disciplined body, the trust in my mind to coordinate and execute — all were gone. People say you don't know it until you lose it. People are right.

My mind could dance. I could imagine the steps, remember how they felt when they happened, see myself in them. My body would betray me. Every plié, each turn, any beginning-level walk across the floor demanded my complete concentration. What didn't hurt was no longer strong. What once had been effortless needed focus almost beyond my ability. I began to wonder about the concert. I needed to dance in it, but I needed to dance brilliantly — to be the best I could be. I was willing to work day and night. I just wasn't sure my body would let me.

I tried to explain myself to Linda at my first rehearsal back. But instead of letting me alone to find my own pace, she made me dance with Sam. In front of everyone. I wasn't ready, but I pushed myself harder than I thought possible. Still, my dance was ugly and uncoordinated, and when they all clapped, I couldn't believe it. I left. It was rude, and I didn't care. I started my car with shaky hands, put it in gear, and jerked away from the curb. I blasted the radio. At the intersection, I didn't see the light change and almost hit a man crossing the street. He glared at me and yelled something obscene, but I just turned away, still shaking. I didn't notice when the light turned green, either. The woman behind honked to get me moving. Finally I was on the freeway for home, but even with the music blaring, the rehearsal kept slamming around my head. What was the matter with everyone? How dare they applaud a lousy performance? Was that supposed to make it all right? Was Linda just trying to let me know I couldn't manage the concert? Or did they really think that feeling sorry for me was "nice"?

My mom was out when I got home. She had left a note saying Rosie had a dance class "recital" at Sunburst and both she and my dad had gone to watch it. I crumpled the paper and, angry, threw it on the floor. They've already done it, I thought — they've traded her for me. The first daughter isn't holding up anymore; thank God we've got a newer one. Maybe this one won't give us so much trouble. This one can still dance. Maybe this one will be normal and grow up like she's supposed to.

I hated her then. I hated all of them. Why couldn't she have cancer? Or my mother? Or my father? Or Linda? Or Sam?

WHY DID IT HAVE TO BE ME?

I could feel my Outside Self losing it. So much control for so long had worn her out, and try as I might to keep her intact and in place, she was slipping.

WHY ME???

Old Outer made a last-ditch attempt to push down the large, wild rage that was working its way up from some cavern where Inside Me was screaming and screaming and screaming and screaming. There was no more hiding from it. No more containment. No more pretense. I was going to die.

Carefully, slowly, precisely, I went into my room and shut the door, then locked it, even though no one was home. Walking deliberately, moving through mud, I stripped off my wet dance clothes and put on a big T-shirt and a pair of shorts. Tenderly, slowly still, I sat down on my bed and drew my legs up close to my chest. I wrapped my arms around them tightly, first the left, then the right. I lowered my head to my knees. My hips and back hurt like hell, but there were no choices left. The explosions that had started inside were big enough and strong enough to break my entire being into molecules and spread them out in the galaxy.

So I held on tight. I closed my eyes and gave myself up to the chaos. Pretending and wish-thinking couldn't stop anything. I could deny, ignore, rage, escape to the Between Place, be calm and clear . . . but this was happening. And it was happening to me. I nodded my acceptance. Then the chaos took over and I hoped I could ride it out. I knew if I eased up even a bit, let my legs slide out a half an inch, turned my head or took a deep breath, there would be no stopping the process. I would cease, utterly and immediately; I would exist only as particles scattered in the sky.

I don't know how long it took, but later came. I was still sitting, stiff now, clutching my legs to my chest. The explosions had finally stopped. I stretched out slowly, mentally probing my body to see what damage had occurred. My arms and hips and knees ached from staying in one position for so long. My eyes were stinging, and I realized I had been crying, too. Crying without even being aware of it. There was no more Outside Me — it had shattered in the rage. Inside Me was cowering still, but a change had come, because Inside Me was now "I" as well. The time for separation had ended.

Who could I rage at because I was dying? Who could I blame? It wasn't anyone's fault. So who should I curse? My parents? They hadn't done it. Fate? What was that? "God" was the only thing big enough to take it on, and I didn't believe in Him.

And why me?

Well. . . . Why not?

Sam

Things were moving even faster now, sliding downhill to who knows where, and the end of high school was imminent. People were obsessing on colleges, summer trips, graduation, and who to take to the prom. The concert was scheduled for the end of April, and the tour would leave the 17th of May. Paul had called and officially ended our relationship by announcing he'd met someone else. And I was having trouble dealing with any of it.

"I'm going to Europe for a year," Brooke announced at least forty times every rehearsal. "After that, Sarah Lawrence or maybe Brown. I got into both, you know."

"One year off from school and I'd never go back," Thea chimed in. "I'm going to University of Colorado. Where the boys are!"

I'd listen and laugh and try to get away before the focus turned to me. Jules and I had always planned to go together to NYU or Santa Cruz, and now, I didn't have a clue what I wanted to do. Besides, I wasn't accepted anywhere. I hadn't mailed the applications. I'd left them in the bottom of my dance bag. My mom went ballistic the night she found them.

"What are these?" she demanded, dropping four sealed, stamped envelopes on my lap.

"Oh. Whoops. I guess I forgot to mail them."

She threw Bruce a look. He smiled and shrugged. He didn't like to get involved in our arguments.

"What did you think you'd be doing next year?"

"Dancing?" I smiled hopefully, but she started shaking her head. "College of Marin?"

"Young lady, if you think I'm going to support you while you hang around doing nothing . . ."

My mouth suddenly lost its connection to my brain. "You don't support me, Mom. Daddy does."

That did it. She went off. She stormed past Bruce, into her room. She peered at me meaningfully as she picked up the porta-phone and dialed. I could hear her mumbling with conviction. Bruce smiled and shrugged again, wishing he could safely walk out. She returned and offered me the phone, grinning triumphantly. "Your father has something to say to you," she announced.

Great, I thought as I took the phone and listened to him lecture on the necessity of going to a good college. They'd finally found something they could agree on.

Then, at school, for the first time in my entire high school career, I got sent to the dean.

"Okay, Samantha," Mr. Watson said, shutting his office door and taking out four disciplinary reports. "What's going on with you?"

"Not much."

"Well, it must be something. You're flunking English, and your ethics teacher complains you can't make it through a single period without mouthing off."

"I'm just contributing to the discussions."

"He finds your contributions a bit derisive."

"Yeah, well, I find his a bit stupid."

He peered at me, smiling a little. "He says you called him a 'flaming asshole.' "

"Okay, so I mouth off once in a while. It's a boring class."

"And English?"

"I guess I'm not doing the homework."

"Does this have anything at all to do with Juliana?"

That was unexpected. "No, not at all."

"I think it might. I'd like you to consider talking with the school psychologist."

"No, thank you."

"Samantha . . ."

"Look, I've been busy with dance, and my boyfriend broke up with me, so I've been a little off. Okay? I'll try to shut up, and I promise to turn in my assignments."

He glared at me. "You're sure that's all?"

"I'm sure."

"If you change your mind, let me know."

"Okay. Can I go?" He nodded and I left.

Because I was home more, the "family situation" intensified, especially the week Bruce went to Tahoe without my mom. She started picking on every little thing I did. And my mouth was still without guidance. When my mom and I fought, I lost the ability to tell when it was time for me to shut up, go and find some homework to do, or just leave the house. I'd lip off. In a big way. Knowing that she'd get the last word in, knowing she'd find a way to get back at me, and knowing she'd make damn sure I was sorry I'd spoken.

One night I was in the bathtub, spacing out, trying to forget my life now and imagining how spectacular it would be when I was out on my own. She poked her head in — no knock, nothing. I knew she was going to continue to bug me about colleges, and I could feel my mouth gearing up.

"Sammie," she started in her whiny voice.

"Do you mind?"

"It'll only take a minute. I —"

"Mother, I'm in the bath."

"I see that. I just want to ask —"

"Later, okay?"

"What is wrong with you?"

"I would just appreciate a little privacy, if you don't mind. I can't seem to get anything else in this house."

"Samantha . . . there's no excuse for this tone of voice."

She was getting mad now, but I couldn't stop. My tone was pitched exactly the way she hated it.

"Get off my goddamn back, okay?"

"I'm going to overlook that last remark. I know you're feeling stressed about graduation, and I know you're upset about Juliana."

That made me crazy.

"Jules is none of your business."

"I'm only trying to —"

"Get a life, why don't you? You're always butting into mine!"

"What?"

"All my friends think you're a real bitch — did you know that?"

"That's it —"

"Nobody likes you. Nobody. Especially not Jules."

"What?!"

"Even Bruce needed a week off."

"You're cruising, kid."

Then I did it. I said the big one.

"Fuck you, Mom."

And not under my breath, either. She looked at me, shook her head, then slammed the bathroom door, hard. A few minutes later she was throwing things around in her room, talking under her breath. I shrugged and got out of the tub, spaciness gone, reality back. I dried off and went to my room. As soon as she knew I was there, she showed up in the doorway.

"All I wanted was tickets for your damn dance concert!"

"So call Linda at the studio."

"Oh, you think I'd go now, huh? After the way you talked to me?"

"Do whatever you like."

"I will, and it'll be a cold day in hell before I go to watch you dance again."

"Fine."

"And I'll just take those car keys, too."

I snatched them off my dresser and dropped them in her hand. "Take whatever you want. I really don't care."

We stood glaring at each other. Then she put her hand over her eyes and took a really big breath.

"I'm sorry." She moved to the dresser and gently put the keys on top. I didn't say anything. "I really don't mean to yell at you, but . . . it comes out. I know you're having a rough time."

I still didn't speak.

"If you want me to come to the concert, I'd be happy to."

"Whatever you like."

She watched me a second more, then left. The second she shut the door, I burst into tears.

Tears! What was my problem? I really didn't care if she saw the show or not. I didn't care about being called in to the dean. I didn't even care if I flunked the stupid English class. But there I was, sitting on the floor of my room, sobbing out of control. I called Brooke but only let it ring twice. Then I dialed Paul's number, listened to him say "Hello," and gently replaced the receiver. I tried to start my English assignment, but I couldn't see the paper through the tears. Finally I called Jules, but her machine answered. I listened to the message, hung up, and called back to listen to it one more time. I fell asleep on top of my covers, still crying, fully dressed.

The days started to roll by, and I focused on the concert to keep from going completely off. I still couldn't stop my mouth. I still burst into tears at the exactly wrong times, and I still cried myself to sleep. But I also rehearsed "The Blues Suite" until I could do it without thinking. And I practiced my part of "The Little Girls' Dance" and made promises to God to do whatever He wanted if only He would let me dance it with Jules.

There was no explanation for anything. People were shifting; relationships were changing right in front of my eyes. Our whole group was uneasy with each other, unsure of who to be now that we were not going to be classmates. People clung tightly to their best friends, letting the others go. Even my mother was acting different. I free-floated and pretended I liked it that way. But late at night, I wished I had my One and Only to hold on to. I wished it were last year, or the year before that. I wished I were anywhere but where I was — hating my last months of high school, hating Paul, hating my mother and father, hating myself.

And mostly hating Jules for being sick.

Julie

My hair waited until two weeks before the concert to fall out. All at once, overnight. I woke with it on my pillow. I didn't scream, but I wanted to. Instead, I took a deep, slow breath. I scooped up the strands, not long, but many, and took them out to the kitchen. From the drawer I took a plastic bag and stuffed the hair inside. My mom came out.

"Good mor— oh, sweetie, oh, honey, I'm sorry."

"Yeah."

"Oh, Julie, come here." She held out her arms to me.

"I can't. Okay? I have to go see Dr. Conner."

"I'll call."

"No, let's just go. She's always there on Mondays."

We got to Campton Medical a couple of hours later. I was wearing my wig and carrying my hair in the bag. When we got up to Pediatrics, my mom had Dr. Conner paged. We waited in her office for her to arrive.

"This is a surprise," she announced as she came in. She looked closely at me, noting the wig. "I hope everything is all right."

My mom looked at me. I stood up and dumped the bag of hair onto her desk.

"You are a liar."

She looked down at the hair and then smiled a little, a sad smile.

"I told you the chances were good —"

"You told me I wouldn't lose my hair."

"Frankly, Juliana, I'm surprised at your priorities."

"You told me I wouldn't lose my hair. You lied."

"You needed the chemotherapy."

"You lied."

"You don't seem to understand what I'm trying to tell you —"

"YOU LIED."

A pause. She looked away. "Yes, I lied."

"You knew I would lose my hair again."

"Yes, but I felt —"

"You knew I wouldn't do the chemo if I was going to lose my hair —"

"Yes, Julie, I did. I also knew that your one chance was to start it again."

I started to cry. I didn't want to, didn't want her to have the satisfaction of seeing my tears.

"I hate you, Dr. Conner. I hate you more than anyone I've ever known."

My mom and I rode home in silence. We pulled up in our driveway, and before I could open the door, she put her hand on my arm.

"I'm proud of you," she said softly. "That was a hard thing to do."

I nodded, not trusting myself to speak. We sat quietly for a moment, and she reached over and touched my face. I leaned my cheek against her hand, and we stayed for years. Finally I whispered, “I'm not going back anymore.”

She sighed.

“I know.”

I looked up and saw the tears in her eyes. She tried to smile at me, but it didn't quite work. Her face was clenched and needing to let go.

“I'm sorry, Mommy.”

She nodded and smiled and started to gently, gently cry. She made soft little kitty noises in her throat, and I could feel my own tears standing behind my eyes, pressing but not falling. I took her hand and kissed it and she leaned into me and I held her. She continued to cry without sound, only the heaving of her shoulders and an occasional deep raspy breath evidence of her pain. I stroked her hair and sang the good-night song she'd made up for me when I was a baby:

I love you when you're happy,
I love you when you're sad
and when you're feeling lonely
or when you're feeling mad.
I love you all the time
in every kind of way.
We'll always be together
Forever and a day.

Finally her sobbing stopped, worn out. She wiped her eyes and her nose on her shirt, then took both my hands and looked straight into my eyes. There were no curtains up for either of us. I knew her in that moment as I knew myself. It almost hurt too much. How long we sat, I couldn't say, but we were startled when there was a knocking on the car window. It was Rosie trying to get our attention. Both of us looked up and were surprised that it was dark.

"Daddy says you guys better come in pretty soon," Rosie announced when we opened the door. She studied us, seeing Mom's teary face, then looked suspiciously at me. "What are you doing out here, anyway?"

I had to miss the final two dress rehearsals for the concert. The blood infection I'd had from the shunt at Christmas had come back off and on since then, and of course it decided to come back now. This time it wouldn't go away. My white cell count was low, and my body couldn't handle it. It was making me too tired to get out of bed, and dancing seemed impossible. I lay and cried and cried. Nothing was going right, and after all the work I'd been doing for the concert, it looked like I was going to miss it after all. My mom called Campton Medical and ended up getting Dr. Conner.

Her suggestion was to bring me into the hospital, hook me up to blood transfusions, and let the new healthy blood help fight the infection. She said I might feel good enough to do the show.

"Call people you know with O-positive blood," she instructed, "and I'll leave orders for immediate delivery. Otherwise it could take forty-eight hours."

The next day I was in the hospital. It seemed best to stay for a few days. Besides getting blood, the nurses could administer drugs for the pain. Morphine was the only thing that kept it manageable since I stopped the chemo for good. Linda had given blood, along with my cousin Eva, my aunt Mary, and Fran, a friend of my mom's. I was scheduled to get two pints the first day and two right before I went to the theater to do the show. After the first one, I began to feel stronger. It was like a miracle — I had energy and I felt good. Even sleep came easy.

The day of the concert, I woke with the first nurse change. Every time a new shift comes on, they have to take your blood pressure and make sure everything is okay. I got my pain medication and a special breakfast. I expected the transfusions to start around ten, so I could leave in the early afternoon and start getting ready for the performance. The way I was feeling, I knew I'd be able to do all the choreography — and do it well.

By eleven, no one had come. I rang for the nurse, and she went to check what was going on.

"There was a multicar collision on Waldo Grade, and most of it ended up here. I don't know what's available as far as your transfusion. We have to treat the emergencies first."

"But there's blood just for me," I told her. "People gave it, specifically."

"Then, okay, you'll be fine. I'm sure they'll get to you as soon as they can."

Lunch came and went. One o'clock, two, three . . . finally, a pair of nurses wheeled in an IV cart. I glared at them.

"Sorry, young lady," the younger one said, "I'm afraid we're going to have to stick you again."

I nodded and held out my arm. He punctured it, taped the needle down, and started the flow. By four o'clock, it was done, but I had to wait another fifteen minutes for the nurse to come back.

"Okay, kid," he said as he unhooked the first bag of blood and started to put on the second.

"You'll have to take this out," I told him, sitting up.

"Excuse me?"

"This needle — I need you to take it out."

"I'm afraid you have another pint indicated here."

"I'll have to do it tomorrow. I have a show tonight."

"Wait —"

"Just please take this out. Or I'll do it myself."

"Let me call your doctor first."

"Okay, fine."

I reached over to where the needle went into my arm.

"I've seen you guys do this enough times. I should be able to, easy."

I started pulling on the tape.

"All right, okay, hold still. I'll do it." He pulled off the tape and took out the needle. "But I'm going to report you to Dr. Conner."

"Go for it. I have to get dressed."

Sam

Linda had just finished telling us who would do what in the show if Jules didn't come when she walked into the theater. We all clapped, and all of a sudden, I knew somehow everything was going to be okay. She'd made it. There was a glimmer in her eye as she looked around at the hugeness of the theater, and I knew she was imagining the whole place filled. I tried to catch her attention as she peeled off her sweats and began to warm up, but she was too intent on whatever was going on in her head and didn't notice.

Jules still danced like nobody else, but it was hard now and you could see it. She didn't push herself during warmup class, like she always used to before a show. She took it easy, stretching enough but not putting out too much energy. Everything was slow-motion, a twitch behind everyone else. When we did the bow sequence as a final warmup, she stood to the side. Linda watched her but didn't insist she dance. After, backstage, as we all sat putting our makeup on, getting dressed and going over last-minute choreography changes, she was quiet. She was there, a part of us and a part of the show, but she was separate at the same time. When we came together for our focus and group hug just before the curtain went up, she lagged back a little and came into the circle last. She stood next to me, and as I put my arm around her, she was so thin I thought she might break.

The show began. Linda had managed to get the Marin Performing Arts Center donated for the night, and since they'd done the publicity, we were performing for an almost full house. It was amazing to be onstage and feel all those bodies, all that human energy out there, just waiting to watch you dance. A full company number started it off, with solo and group parts that wove in and out of each other. Jules had decided not to do this one so she could handle the next dance, a piece to Sting's "King of Pain." It was excruciatingly hard, mostly floor work and slow, controlled turns and balances. I watched her from the wings. Her concentration was total. Her absolute immersion in the music drew your eye. Three other really good dancers were dancing, but I saw only her.

I was on next in an up-tempo jazz piece. As I danced, I noticed Jules backstage, leaning on the wall, head down. She was breathing hard, holding on to herself, all alone. I wanted to go to her, to see if she was all right, but there was no place in the dance that allowed me to get off and then back on. I went into the part with chaîné turns and steps facing upstage, and when I glanced back, she was gone. I figured she had got it together. I found out later, from Brooke, that she'd had to be helped off the stage.

Still she came on for her next number. She smiled, she danced, she played with the audience and made them smile with her enthusiasm and her energy. Offstage, she almost collapsed. At intermission, I found her in the bathroom, sitting on the toilet, running a cold, wet towel over the back of her neck.

"It's okay if you don't want to do 'The Little Girls' Dance,' you know. Sarah and Colleen have been rehearsing it. You could rest and then, you know, come on for the finale."

"I'm fine." She didn't look up.

"Are you sure?"

"I'm fine."

Twenty minutes later, we took our places for our dance. Sitting on the stage, holding hands, in the pose from a children's game, we looked across at each other. I smiled, hoping she'd respond, and she did. She smiled back, and then she winked. For a second, a tiny second, nothing was wrong. We were together, my One and Only and me — right where we belonged. The music began, and so did we, trusting each other, in sync with life, giving everything we could. In the final moments, as she pointed to the "ribbon" coming down, and I reached to catch it, there was that same wash of silence. As the curtain started to close, the applause began. It was so loud and so demanding, the stage manager signaled for us to take another bow. It was too late, though — Jules had left the stage. Sarah and Brooke called for her, but she didn't come back. I bowed alone.

The show was a hit. We had our money for our tour. Linda rushed around backstage and hugged us all. We hugged each other, laughing and congratulating ourselves, exalted that we had actually met our goal. The tour was a reality, and we had done it!

"Let's go to Mim's and party!" Sarah suggested.

"Screw Mim's — let's go to the city!" said Brooke.

"Yeah, come on, guys — we deserve it," Colleen offered.

"I'll drive!" I said.

"Me, too!" said Thea. "Come on! There's a great place in North Beach!"

"Parteee!!" came from all over the room.

"Wait . . . we hafta all go together," Sarah insisted. That's when I noticed Jules was quietly leaving the room, dance bag over her shoulder.

"Wait a minute, Jules — you have to come, too," I said. Suddenly the room got completely quiet. One of us wouldn't be going on the tour.

She shook her head and smiled. "I don't think I better. I'm pretty tired."

"Oh, come on!" "You can!" "Please, Julie . . ." Everyone flocked around her, pleading.

"Thanks, guys. But I'm going home."

No one looked at each other after she left, just finished their dressing and packing up without any words. I followed her out through the crowd. People smiled at me and said "good show," and I nodded back, enjoying the recognition. I called to Jules as we got outside, but she didn't turn around. I know she heard me — her shoulders went up a little and she shook her head — but she didn't want to respond. There was nothing else I could do, so I went back inside. Later, I went with Brooke to a restaurant in Sausalito, overlooking the bay. We had a wonderful time. We managed not to talk about Jules at all.

Julie

I couldn't remember most of the show. Not really. Not the way I used to remember dancing. The moments, the isolated areas of reaching past where you used to reach. Feeling that audience in front of you, who you sensed more than saw because of the lights . . . knowing they were there and drawing more and more than you ever thought you could give. And the moments of funny, the times you missed something and covered, or ended up somewhere you weren't supposed to be. The nervousness before curtain, the exhilaration after . . . none of it happened. At least not for me.

What I did remember was the urgency of needing to leave the clinic to get to the theater on time. The new blood had made me feel a little better, a little stronger, but it was only temporary, and I had to get going while I still could. Arriving at the theater, backstage before we started, and even the dances themselves were a blur. I couldn't define them. Only feel how difficult they were.

Never in my life have I worked as hard. Each count of eight seemed endless, every part of each step harder than the last. The audience was hungry and sucking every last bit of effort out of me. They didn't think I could do it. No one thought I could. Not my parents, not Linda, not even Sam. It wasn't important. I was dancing for myself because I promised myself I would, because I couldn't not dance. It didn't matter what anyone else thought or felt. This was for me, and I didn't care what the cost was. Besides, no one really saw me anymore. My road had not only veered out by itself — it had gotten lost in the forest. I had almost completely disappeared.

Except to Rosie. When she looked, I was still there. Maybe she wasn't old enough to start looking through me, to pretend to ignore what I had become. She just saw me. Every time I came on the stage, she yelled out, in her high, squeaky voice, "Julsie! I see my Julsie!" The same as always. And I could hear people laughing, the same as always. Except now it wasn't cute.

Now it made me mad. And every time she yelled "Julsie," I got madder. Uncontrollably. By the time the show was over, I was furious with her, and with my parents for letting her do it. Backstage, I pulled off my leotards and dressed quickly, ignoring all the hoopla that was going on around me. Everyone was celebrating because the company could now go on tour; our show had made the money we needed. They seemed to forget that I wasn't going, and almost that I was even there. Until Sam noticed. Then they all turned and stared. In a moment they realized their omission and started crowding around. High from the show, for the completion of their goal, they looked right at me and didn't see a thing. I was fading, and they didn't even notice.

"Come with us!" they all begged.

I wanted to scream at them, but I didn't have the energy. I wanted to slap Sam for bringing me to their attention. She was just like Rosie — she couldn't let me be. Somehow I made my excuses without raising my voice; somehow I got out of the dressing room. I went through the theater, and no one, not one person in the entire crowd waiting for the dancers, stopped me to say "good show" or "great dancing." Even though I was holding my Company bag and wearing my Company sweatshirt. Even though many of them recognized me. I heard Sam call, but I didn't turn around. She stopped following as I went into the parking lot, where my parents were waiting. The night had turned cold, but I didn't feel it. The effects of the blood transfusion had worn off completely, and I was barely making myself walk.

Rosie came running up, excited, happy, energetic, and healthy. My parents were smiling, obviously proud, and I knew they were eager to congratulate me. My dad held his video camera. I glared at them.

"Couldn't you keep the little brat quiet?" I asked my mom. "She ruined the whole show."

Rosie stopped like she'd been slapped and hid her face behind my mom's leg. Tears came into her eyes, and her lips started to quiver. I tried unsuccessfully to control my voice.

"Do we have to stand here looking stupid? Could we please go home?"

My father and mother looked at each other, almost sheepishly, and my dad pointed behind me.

"You drove yourself, honey," he said.

"I know! Don't you think I know that?" I yelled at him.

"Julie . . ." My mom started to reach for me. I pushed her away.

"Don't you people understand anything? I can't drive

home! I can't dance, I can't think, I can't do anything anymore!"

I was out of control, and I knew it. I knew other people in the parking lot were looking over, staring, but I didn't know how to stop.

"Is everybody in this whole family stupid? I've got fucking cancer — don't you know that? Why do you expect me to drive myself home!?"

There was a long, horrible moment when no one spoke or moved. I glared at my parents, and they stared helplessly back at me. Then a wave of dizziness hit, and I reached out for my mom. She grabbed me and held me and, with a glance at my dad, started toward their car. Rosie refused to be near me, so my dad took her with him, in my car. She stared at me from the backseat as they pulled out of the parking lot.

My mom put her hand on my leg. I moved away.

"Julie, honey . . . ," she said softly. I shook my head. I was too angry. I couldn't speak. I couldn't even listen. We drove the rest of the way in silence.

At home, my mom helped me in, then took a sullen, pouty Rosie to her bedroom. My dad retreated to the den. I sat at the dining room table and tried to figure out where it had all gone wrong. Nothing had been what I'd hoped — and now it was over. I looked up. My mom was watching from the doorway. She smiled. I realized my anger had faded. But the emptiness that had taken its place felt even worse.

"Want a back rub?" my mom asked.

I shook my head no.

"Want to talk about it?"

I shook my head again. I had no more feelings. How could I have any words?

"I just want to go to bed," I told her, and let her walk me to my room. She helped me change, kissed me good night, and tucked me in. Even though I knew I wouldn't sleep, I closed my eyes. After a few moments, I heard her gently shut the door.

After everyone else dropped off, I went outside on the deck and sat there in my nightgown. It was dark and very cold. I made myself still, letting the coldness slice through me and feeling the slight wind on my cheeks, tracing my tears. The concert was done. There was no chance I'd be able to make the tour. I'd barely had the strength for the few dances I'd done tonight. Besides, I had to get blood transfusions and antibiotics and whatever else whoever decided should be pumped into me. I wasn't sure why.

I tried to save the night, but not enough could be captured. No moments presented themselves, and I wondered if maybe, just maybe, I *was* disappearing. If when I'd walked through the crowd at the end of the night, they hadn't been ignoring me . . . I simply couldn't be seen. Maybe only Rosie saw me now because Rosie was going to have to take my place.

I closed my eyes, not sleeping. The cold didn't feel as bad now, or maybe I was too cold on the inside for it to matter. I tried to find an avenue to send my thoughts so I could focus a little bit, figure out what was going on, understand why I was either feeling too much or nothing at all. It didn't work. In back of my eyes were nightmare colors, swirling around and colliding in dark, violent, ugly patterns. I tried to change it. I wanted to get away from it, from me. I wanted to scream, to run, to smash my head into a concrete wall and not have to think about anything anymore. I was tired of having to work so hard. Tired of pain and shots and faces with stupid expressions. Of knowing more than I ever wanted to about cancer and chemo and doctors and dying.

I started to cry, the slow, leaky kind that can absolutely not be stopped no matter what you try to do. No sound anywhere, just snot in my nose and more tears on my face. I didn't brush them away. They dripped off my chin and fell to my chest, and I sat feeling it all. Then an enormous fear descended, banishing my nightmare colors and freezing my tears, making my breathing snatchy and brittle, smashing through everything I ever was or knew or thought. I couldn't stop it, couldn't grasp it, and couldn't escape it.

What was it going to be like? What would I feel? What would I think? Would I know what was happening to me, or would I just stop being aware and not even realize it, like when you get anesthesia before an operation? Was I right about reincarnation? Was there a God waiting to punish me, to decide if I went to heaven or to hell? Or was there nothing? Would it hurt? Would I know what to do and how to do it?

I thought of Jack's dad, in the hospital before he died. I thought of my dog, Jonti, who got hit by a car when I was seven and had to be put to sleep. My uncle Eddie had died, and a three-year-old second cousin I had seen only once. People did it every day. How could it be that hard? The fear started backing off a little, then circled around and ambushed me from behind. It didn't matter who else had done it; this time it was me. And I would have to do it all alone.

All of a sudden, with my eyes wide open, with no question about being completely awake, I saw my almost scary-looking old man. He'd sat with me so many times in my Between Place. Now he was floating in front of me, and for the first time, I looked directly at him. His eyes were serious and deep and unbearably gentle. He spoke and I heard him, without a word being uttered or a sound made. He held my hands without touching me, kissed my forehead without coming near. A wash of peacefulness and calm settled around me. I could taste it and hear it and almost touch it; it came from inside and out simultaneously. I asked him my questions, and they were answered. I nodded at him. He waited a breath, cocked his head to one side, and sort of smiled, then nodded back. I took a long, good, deep breath. Finally, as the sun was beginning to rise, I must have dropped off.

"Julie, honey, come on — let's go in," my mother was saying. "It's freezing out here. Let's get you in bed."

I came awake immediately. Everything hurt, but my mind was clear. "Mom . . . Mom, I want to go to the banquet."

"What?" She sort of chuckled. She was used to me being incoherent when I first woke up.

"To the company's tour kickoff banquet, you know? I want to go."

She stared at me for a minute and shook her head. "Honey, I really don't think —"

"You don't understand. I'm going to go."

"Let's talk about it later, when you've rested."

I slept for almost four hours and was no less sure of it when I woke. The banquet was almost three weeks away, the day before the company was scheduled to board the plane for L.A., and I was determined to go. I realized now that the banquet was the other part of the show for me. I had finished my dancing and now, I needed to finish . . . what? I couldn't say it in words, I just knew it was the right thing to do. My parents tried to talk me out of it. They were rational; I was adamant. They were pushy; I was quietly serious. They appealed to my sensible self; I ignored them. Finally they forbade me to go. I threw a tantrum.

"She's going to hurt herself doing that!" my father yelled as I cried and screamed and raged on the living room couch. "Stop her!"

"You stop her!" my mother yelled back. "You're the one who said she couldn't go."

"Julie . . . Juliana!" my dad said, trying to be heard over my noise. "It's okay, stop this now. . . . If it means that much, you can go to the banquet."

I stopped. I knew I would get my way.

Sam

With the concert over and the tour still a few weeks away, the dean informed me that I wouldn't be allowed to graduate if I didn't bring up my grades. My mother followed up with a real threat: "No grades — no tour." I couldn't escape. I still didn't have a clue what I would do after graduation, but that didn't seem to matter.

Studying at home was a drag, so I ended up spending my evenings at the Mill Valley Library. I saw Rachael and Jack there sometimes, but we never spoke. Then one night, Rachael joined me at the table. I looked at her with surprise.

"I know. I don't like you, either," she told me. "But Jack needs to talk to you. It's really important." She gestured toward him, sitting by himself near the door. He got up abruptly and went outside.

"So let him come over and talk."

"He won't. He's afraid of you."

"Oh, come on!"

"Shhhhh!" an old man warned from the next table. Rachael continued in whispers.

"Please? It won't take long."

I came close to a smart reply, but something in her voice made me pause.

"Is it about Jules?"

"Sort of. But mostly it's about Jack."

With the old man glaring at us, I followed Rachael outside. Jack was sitting on a bench in front of Old Mill Park. Rachael stopped on the library porch, and I walked over by myself. He looked as if he'd been crying.

"You don't have to say anything," he told me, blinking and sniffing as he talked. "Just listen."

"Okay."

"My dad was in the hospital for two weeks after he had the first heart attack — you remember?" I didn't, but I nodded. "And Julie kept telling me I needed to go see him. She kept saying, 'It's really important to say you love him. Just in case.' " He wiped his face on his sleeve and continued. "But I didn't do it. I only went there when he was sleeping, so I wouldn't have to talk to him." Rachael came up to us, sat down, and put her arm around Jack. There was no sound but his stifled crying. Finally he looked up at me. "I never told him, Sammie. And then he died."

Something broke inside me then, and I had to turn and walk away. Grabbing my books from the library, I threw them in the back of the car and started driving up Mount Tam, away from my house and Jules and Jack and everything else. Just past Mountain Home, halfway up, I pulled over to the side and got out. Where was I going? The road would just go over the top and back down the other side. I walked a bit up the hiking trail and sat in the dark on the edge of a bluff. I could see Mill Valley down below.

I remembered the first time Jules and I had shaved our legs.

"It's no big deal," I'd insisted as we hid in her bathroom with my mom's old razor. "You just push down and swoop it up."

Then I demonstrated, cutting off a strip of skin all the way up the center of my leg. I stood there, speechless, watching the blood well up. Jules doused me with half a bottle of hydrogen peroxide and tried to stuff a towel in my mouth to keep me from yelling. Sandra found us anyway.

Then there was the first time we tried drinking. It was the summer before ninth grade. We'd been sneaking alcohol from the places we baby-sat and storing it in a jelly jar in the back of my closet. Everything was mixed together — bourbon, gin, vodka. We didn't know the difference. We snuck it into a dance at San Rafael High. We hid in the bathroom, held our noses, and drank the whole nasty thing. Then we walked out onto the dance floor.

"Damn, I don't feel a thing," Jules said.

"Me, either. Maybe you're not supposed to mix it."

Then the floor tipped, and the rest of the dance was a blur of images and uncontrollable giggling.

The night my father left for good, I called Jules at two in the morning. My mom hadn't come home, and I didn't know what else to do. She and Sandra came over and picked me up. Sandra tucked us both in Jules's bed, and I cuddled in her arms and cried until I finally fell asleep.

Then I remembered the day we'd met. It was in a dance class, of course. I was nine and taking ballet from Margarete at The Belrose, where the company now rehearsed. I wasn't very good yet, but I imagined myself to be the next Gelsey Kirkland. Then Jules came. She'd studied with the San Francisco Ballet, but the commute for classes had gotten too much, so Sandra had brought her to The Belrose.

I could picture exactly how she looked: her hair in a tight little bun on the back of her head, white leotard, pink tights and shoes, carrying a small black dance bag. We all gave her the once-over as she quietly took her place at the barre.

I smiled arrogantly. The class had been together for months, and we were right in the middle of learning a difficult variation. I knew she'd never get it, and I knew how stupid she was going to feel. For about two minutes, anyway. Then we all could see how strong her technique was and how hard she worked. Not only did she get the variation, she knew the ending, and Margarete had her demonstrate it for the class.

I hated her. She moved up a level immediately, and I started my campaign. I added classes, I worked at home, and I begged for a chance to move up, too. Margarete finally agreed. Then, when the spring concert came around, she gave us a pas de deux to perform. We'd rehearse it for two hours after our Saturday class, each of us trying our best to outdance the other, and in performance, we were brilliant. The breakthrough came when the cast watched the videotape the week after the show. Jules and I were absolutely stunning together onstage. Even we could see it. Light and Dark, Day and Night, Sun and Moon. I remembered exactly how we smiled at each other for the first time. Pretty soon, you couldn't keep us apart. In fact, there wasn't a thing I had done since then that didn't involve Jules in some way or another.

Until now.

The next day I cut school. I was flunking anyway, so it was no big deal. I drove to her house, parked across the street, and finally got out of the car and knocked on the door. Sandra let me in, and I could tell she was really glad to see me. We didn't talk, just hugged; then she took me into the den. Jules was sitting on the couch in her old blue robe, watching a talk show on TV. At least she had the TV turned on. Her eyes were closed.

"Hey, Jules!"

She turned her head toward me, slowly . . . slowly . . . slowly. Her wig was off, and her hair, almost an inch long, was covered loosely by a scarf. When she saw me, she tried to smile. But something was wrong. I turned to ask Sandra, but she'd left. I looked back, not meaning to stare, but I couldn't help it. Up close, her face was distorted. Her left eye was pulling down, and she couldn't smile on that side.

"It's a tumor," she said in someone else's voice. "On my brain."

"Shit, Jules," I answered, before I realized what I was saying. "Oh, I'm sorry." She tried to smile.

"Same old Sam."

So much had changed in so little time. When she talked, her voice was soft, weak. Her words were slurred, slow, carefully formed.

"Does it hurt?" I asked.

"No, not the tumor."

"How 'bout the rest of you?"

"Yeah, I guess. But it's okay. I give myself shots."

I nodded, not knowing how to respond. In the quiet that followed, I was aware of her breathing. It sounded rough and uncomfortable. Jules was looking down and apologized for it, saying she was dizzy most of the time from the tumor and the medication. I nodded again, knowing she didn't see me. All of a sudden she looked up, into my eyes. Her mouth was trying to keep the rest of her face from crying.

"Dr. Conner lied. She told me my hair wouldn't fall out."

I nodded, and my own tears started. Jules reached out her hand; I covered it with mine.

"She's a shithead," I whispered finally.

"A dickface," she said in her slow words.

"The daughter of swine."

"May she get boils in her eyelids."

"I hope her asshole closes up."

Then we laughed. It was a quick one, but it felt good. We sat quietly for a while. Jules nodded off a little. I realized my heart had slowed and my head was no longer pounding. I watched her as she dozed, waited easily until she woke again.

"Hey, sleepyhead, you wanna go for a ride?"

"No, thanks."

"Come on — I'll drive slow."

"No. I'm not very strong right now."

"You wanna go or not?"

"Not."

"Come on — it'll do you good."

"Sam, I don't think so."

"We can go to Brooke's mom's beach house. I know where they hide the key."

"Well . . ."

"Come on . . ."

"I don't know . . ."

"Please, Jules?"

"Okay, but I can't walk too good."

Jules leaned on me and Sandra as we went to the car, and I watched to see exactly how Sandra lowered her into the seat. I wanted to be able to help her later on. She sat quietly all the way through Mill Valley and up Mount Tam. There wasn't much traffic, and the air was nice. When we got to Brooke's house, I went for the key, then opened the house up and helped her inside.

Empty of people, in the clear light of morning, the place was even more amazing. The windows facing the ocean made you feel you were in space, suspended there with only the deck outside to hold you up. The living room kind of exploded around you. The ceilings were high, all open and light, and two large splotches of purple-blue art faced each other on the walls. No furniture anywhere — only several thick rugs, and the swimming pool. Yes, the wonderful swimming pool, right in the middle of the house. The bottom was painted the same purple-blue as the art on the wall.

Jules looked like she'd come home.

We didn't talk. She sat on the middle rug, and I opened three of the five huge sliding glass doors that were the outside wall. A cold sea breeze and the sound and smell of the ocean immediately filled the room. I found some pillows and a blanket and brought them over, helping Jules prop herself up. I sat down near her, and we just simply tried to take it all in.

The sky was losing its clearness. It was not quite yet overcast but wanting to be. The wind was strong, gusting and chilled. Gulls were all over the place, sliding around the air, then swooping for fish. One landed on the deck outside, face into the wind, chest extended with head slightly back, defiant and ready. Another joined him, then another and another. Seventeen gulls landed, all of them facing the same way — into the wind, chests out, heads back. Jules and I dared not move. Suddenly one gull took off, soaring, then two more, then three in a group, another by itself, another group of four. All took to the skies, the last one ascending as a new one landed — same direction, same pose. The choreography was spectacular.

In another instant, they were all back, and the pattern was repeated again, and again, and a fourth time. Then they all took off. We waited, delighting in this unexpected show, but none came back. After a long moment, we looked over at each other, smiling and amazed, disappointed that it had come to an end. Then Jules pointed, and I turned to see one gull, by herself, staring in through the open door. The wind at her side ruffled her feathers, and she wobbled a little. Then nodded. Yes, I swear — she nodded. Just one time. I thought I saw Jules nodding back. Then she flew away.

We stayed several hours at Brooke's, not talking about anything, really. Mostly we watched the skies, and then when it warmed up a little, we sat outside and watched the water. I rummaged in the kitchen and came up with enough healthy food that Jules could eat and not have to return home for a meal.

"It's not cooked very well," I told her as I brought it out. "You know I'm for shit in the kitchen."

"As long as I can get it down."

"We'll see."

While she ate, I watched her. But I watched as if I were far, far away and seeing things only from a telescope. I was there and yet I wasn't. She ate very deliberately, placing each piece in her mouth and chewing it slowly. She only managed half. I took the plate to the kitchen, washed it, and came back to the deck. She had moved to a wide chaise lounge. She patted it when I came back, and I sat down next to her and pulled my legs up underneath me. We looked out over the ocean.

"'Member when we talked about what happens?" she asked.

It took a minute for me to realize what she was asking about, and I almost but not quite felt uncomfortable.

"Uh-huh."

"Did you think anymore about it?"

"Yeah, I guess I did."

"What do you think? Do you think I was right?"

"You mean about going to another awareness, and then coming back, and all that stuff?"

"Mmm-hmm."

"Yeah, I think so."

"Really? Really, truly?"

"Yeah."

"Tell me."

"What I think?"

"Mmm-hmm."

"Well, I guess I believe the only thing that really gets changed is your body. I mean, it . . . you know, dies. But you don't. Not the real part, the *you* part . . . you know, the soul or whatever you'd call it."

She nodded and took all that in, and when she spoke again, I could hardly hear her.

"Do you think it hurts?"

I waited a minute before answering, thought about it. I wanted to make sure I believed what I was about to say. She watched my face but didn't speak.

"No. I don't think it hurts at all."

"For true?"

"For true."

She nodded.

"I think you're right."

She paused, looked straight into my eyes and tried to smile. "It's now that hurts."

"Yeah."

She leaned over, into me, and I put my arm around her. Her weight was nothing, her body almost nonexistent. She dropped her hand on my lap. As I covered it with my own, I marveled. Everything else had been changed by the cancer — her face, her hair, her body — but those long fingers, those delicate dancer hands, were untouched, and exquisitely beautiful.

Julie

Time started to slow down, or speed up. I'm not sure. Nothing and everything happened. I changed without moving. I traveled miles without leaving my house. My body was shutting down, but not my mind. I listened to the world and watched my road veer off farther in its solo direction. The ghosts who were my mother and father and Rosie and Sam floated in and out with the ghosts of people I didn't know. Sometimes I'd hear them crying. Sometimes they'd speak and I'd reply. Other times, I'd ignore them. I'd be off laughing in the clouds with my wonderful almost scary old man. The distance was growing, and I was getting ready. And I knew the banquet was coming soon.

Once? Maybe more . . . Rosie slipped into my room and stood by my bed, looking. I sensed her more than saw her; opening my eyes these days was often unbearable. Reaching out might have scared her, and it was too hard to speak. What did she see? Did she even realize who I was, or had I changed so much that she couldn't remember me anymore? I wished I had been nicer to her. I wished I could connect, just once more, like we used to do when she was younger, before I'd gotten sick. I drifted away. She slipped her hand under mine and with her other hand, curled my fingers around hers. I opened my eyes and tried to look at her, tried to make my face smile. I don't know if it worked, but at least she didn't run out. We looked at each other, into each other. Her face was mine. She stroked my cheek, just once. I drifted away again. She was gone when I came back.

Sam

No one could believe it when Jules showed up at the restaurant where we were having our kickoff banquet. But there she was, just as we finished eating, all dressed up and in this huge wheelchair. Her mom and dad wheeled her in, and for a long scary moment, not one person spoke. Then Linda stood and started applauding, and we all joined in. Jules rolled her eyes and dropped her head down, smiling that crooked smile. She held up her hand for us to stop, but we clapped on and on, standing up and getting the attention of the entire place.

Finally we stopped, and Linda made room at the head of the table. Sandra wheeled Jules up close. Still, no one knew what to say. We all kept smiling, and I know we were all thinking the same thing. This tiny person, this elf-creature with an oversize wig and practically no body; how could this be Juliana? Her face was old and her expressions contorted by the tumor.

"I hope you don't mind that I came," she said. Her voice was barely there, light and wispy. She had to pause every few words to catch her breath. "I wanted to say 'break a leg' before you go." She paused, waiting, but no one spoke. She looked around the table, smiling at each person. “Hey guys, it’s still me. I promise.” Still no response. “I could go home if you don’t want me here.”

We fell over each other to make her know we did want her, and the evening got back to normal. Then, somehow, in the next hour, Jules found time alone with each dancer in the company, holding a hand out for her to take and listening carefully to her words. Then Jules would speak, and even though I couldn’t hear what she said, each person came away changed somehow, a little bigger, a little deeper, touched by their moment with her. I watched her from my seat, so proud of her, so amazed by this effort. Her parents watched, too, their smiles never for one instant leaving. When she came to me, no words were needed. We held hands and locked eyes. Then, before we knew it, it was over.

Outside, as we were all saying good-bye, Linda called all the dancers together. We made a circle like we do before every performance, and Sandra wheeled Jules into her place. We took hands.

“I just want to say to Julie that we’ll miss you on this tour. You should be going with us, and I hate that you’re not. You are an incredible, inspirational young woman, and I love you very much. We all do. And so we are dedicating our work this next week to you. All of it. We will be dancing for you, even if you won’t get to see it, except in the video. We’re calling it ‘The Juliana Tour.’ ” She smiled. “I hope that’s okay.”

Jules nodded. She was crying softly and didn’t try to speak. She didn’t have to.

Sandra came over, and before she took Jules away, I leaned over and kissed her on the cheek. She touched my face and mouthed, “I love you.” Then we stood as a company and watched her go.

✡ ✡ ✡

The next morning we were at the San Francisco Airport bright and early. I hadn't slept more than a few hours the night before, wavering between the excitement of going on tour and the fullness left over from seeing Jules. Wearing our company jackets, feeling like a professional group of dancers, we hung out rather importantly in the main terminal, waiting for our flight to be called. Never before had we felt so much a group, an entity, and most of it was because of Jules. She had given us the focus we'd been lacking. We had a purpose; we were "The Juliana Tour."

"United flight 1729 to Los Angeles will begin boarding at gate 74A," said the loudspeaker.

We gathered our dance bags and our carry-on luggage and started toward the gate. Going through the security check outside the waiting area, I heard my name.

"Samantha Russell, please pick up the white courtesy telephone. Samantha Russell, the white courtesy telephone, please."

I looked over at Linda, who shrugged, puzzled. Handing my bags to Sarah and Brooke, I pushed back through the lines and found a white telephone. Picking it up, I gave my name. A minute later, I heard Sandra on the phone. My stomach contracted.

"Oh, Sammie, good, I'm glad I caught you —"

"What? What is it?"

"I think you should come back."

"Okay." My heart thumped in my chest.

"Julie went into a coma last night. Will you come down to the hospital?" She paused. "I think you might want to say good-bye."

"Okay," I said, feeling my mouth go dry and my insides evaporate. "Okay, okay. I will."

"It's Campton Medical, in her same room. But I don't want you coming alone. Is there someone there who can drive you?"

"Okay, yes, sure."

Somehow, and I will never be able to say exactly how, because I can't remember anything but the pounding that was going on in my head and the way I could feel my heart beating, I got back to Linda and the girls and I told them what Sandra had said. Linda took charge immediately, talking first to the ticket agent and her supervisor, then giving instructions to the girls to go home and wait for her call. I don't remember what she said, only their faces, changing.

Then we were walking through the airport and outside to the shuttle bus. Linda held my arm as we boarded it and rode to the parking garage. I was conscious of each minute, each person that came and went in my sight, and everything that Linda said. It was all surrounded by a haze, though, outlined by this grayish fog that made it seem stark and over-real in contrast. Linda didn't try to talk much, but she didn't let go of my hand, either. We got off the shuttle and found her car, waited forever at the gate to pay, and finally got on the road. We got to the hospital less than an hour after Sandra had first called.

I knew the place too well and walked now through the maze with confidence. Linda came with me, down the hall, up the elevator to Pediatrics, around the corner to the room that had become "Julie's room" because she'd stayed there so often. I recognized several of the nurses, and they smiled sadly at me. I saw Dr. Conner and ignored her.

Sandra was standing just outside the room, talking in a low voice with her sister and another woman. William was just walking out and saw me first. As I got closer, he came up and grabbed me, holding me very tight. He started to cry, big gulping scary sounds, and asked me over and over, "What are we going to do, Sammie? What are we going to do?"

I held him back, but I didn't know what to say. Sandra took my hand, and we stood there until her sister moved him away, walking him down the hall and around the corner. I vaguely noticed Linda waiting a short distance down the hall.

"Julie went to sleep on the way home from the banquet," Sandra said, holding my hand to her and stroking the back of it, "and she never really woke up. We brought her here this morning, about three. The doctors say she's, um, probably not going to come back."

I looked at Sandra. She tried to smile. Her voice was even and low, and her eyes were dry. Only the tightness of her mouth exposed any of what she was feeling inside.

"I think it's time for all of us to tell her good-bye." Her voice was soft but strong.

I shook my head no and started to cry. Sandra pulled me around gently to face her. She held my face in her hands and came close. I looked in her eyes and saw her determination.

"Not now, Sammie. You can't cry right now. Okay?"

I nodded, but still I couldn't stop the tears. She took my hands and gave a little shake.

"Sammie, listen, please. This time is for Julie. She needs you, and you have to pull yourself together. I don't want her to leave to the sound of our crying. Okay?"

I nodded and sniffed, and took a long, deep breath. When I was ready, Sandra led me to the door.

"I *know* she can hear you," she told me. "The doctors

say not, but I don't believe them. So you just let her know how much you love her."

I nodded again and went into the room.

Sandra walked around one side of the bed, and I went to the other. There was no sound but Jules breathing, loud and slow, each breath in and out harsh and labored. She was so very small in the bed, like a little girl. Her face was peaceful, except for an anguished expression that would pass over it every once in a while. Her eyes were closed, and she wasn't wearing her wig. The distortion her tumor had caused was relaxed. Her mouth opened slightly with her breathing. She looked beautiful.

I took her hand, still lovely and untouched. Sandra had painted her nails a baby pink.

"Hi, you." Her fingers rested lightly in mine. I stroked her softly, up her arm and down.

"I'm going to leave you guys alone for a few minutes," Sandra said, and went out the door.

All of a sudden, I was scared. I wanted to run away, to go back to the airport or take a dance class or anything to stop this from happening. It couldn't be real. This couldn't be my best friend. But it was, and I didn't know what to do. I wanted to say the right things, but I didn't know what they were. I kept stroking her arm.

"You look so beautiful, Jules. You look so beautiful. I love you very much."

A big lump came up in my throat and a tear out of my eye. She groaned softly, startling me. She moved her head back and forth a few times, and I felt her hand tighten on mine. Just a little, but definitely a tightening. Sandra was right; she *could* hear me. And even though she didn't have a way of speaking, she was letting me know we were there together. The walls went away. I remembered who we were.

"You're my One and Only, Jules. You are. Now and always, wherever we are, whatever happens. And I'm your Other Self. I don't know why it happened like that, but it did. And I love you. And I'm sorry if I haven't been the best friend I could, but . . . well, I'm sorry."

"She waited for you, you know." Sandra's voice startled me. She had never completely left the room. "The doctors thought she'd be gone by this morning, but I knew she had to wait."

"I don't understand."

"She can't leave until you tell her good-bye. I did already, and her daddy did. But she needs you to let her go, too."

The tears hit the back of my eyes, and I blinked frantically to keep them from coming out. Jules's hand was still in mine, and I had to ease off squeezing it.

"I wish I could talk to her."

"You are."

"Yeah, but she's not talking back."

"Yes, she is. Just not in words."

I knew she was right. I could feel it.

"I'm going to miss her."

"She knows."

"I don't know what I'm going to do without her."

"She knows that, too. Now you have to say good-bye."

"I don't know if I can."

"Look at her, Sammie. We can't hold her here, not like this. She's had so much pain, for so long. She deserves to be free of it."

"I don't know what to do."

"I know."

I looked back at my friend. Her breathing was harsher now, and a bit of saliva glistened at the corner of her mouth. I reached down with my free hand and dabbed it away. I had never in my life felt older or heavier than I did at that moment.

I stroked her face. I leaned over and kissed her lightly on the forehead, then on her lips. I smoothed the short hair back and held her hand to my face.

"Good-bye, my dancer, my friend, my One and Only. I love you."

I stayed in the hospital with Jules and Sandra and the family for the rest of that day and all of the night. We sat in her room; we walked with each other down the hallways and back; once I went to the cafeteria and tried unsuccessfully to eat something. Different people came and went. Linda and Brooke and Sarah came, and I led them into the room, assured them Jules could hear them, and then stood holding her hand while they talked. I don't know what they said. I really couldn't listen.

Pretty soon it was only me and the family left. It got easier to talk to her, but she didn't respond again. She seemed to be farther and farther away. Her breathing got heavier and slower; sometimes it stopped for a few minutes. We would all look at each other, and we would stop breathing, too. The silence would be overpowering. Then she would start the sound again — labored, raspy, hard. And we would be relieved and at the same time angry.

William asked the question. "My poor baby. Why is it so hard for her to let go?"

I couldn't say it, but I knew why. Jules could do nothing without doing it completely. In her dancing, in her relationships with other people, she always tried harder, stayed longer, and gave more. Why would this next step be any different?

At about six the next morning, she decided to leave. I was in the family waiting room down the hall, asleep on the chair. Her father slept nearby, fitfully. Sandra came in and put her hand on my arm. I woke instantly.

"She's gone, Sammie."

I looked at her, blankly at first and then with a huge sigh that came out of my feet and up through my body. I nodded. I could feel the tears in the back of my face, but they weren't ready yet. It was too real, too close to me, too damn big. All I could do was nod.

"I think you should come home with us," Sandra whispered. "If that's okay with you."

I nodded again. This was probably what I would be doing for the rest of my life, I thought — nodding. I didn't seem capable of anything else. Sandra went to her husband, to the father of Jules, and shook him gently. No words here. He just looked at her, and she tried to smile as she took his hand, and he started to cry. Big tears, huge gulping noises, a man not used to this act; he was clumsy with it, and loud. I felt uncomfortable with his newness. I felt impossible with the truth.

How we got to Jules's house, I don't know. I suppose Sandra drove. Rosie was awake when we arrived, her big brown eyes looking too much like her sister's. She knew. She didn't know what — but she knew. She didn't ask where Julie was, and she didn't come near any of us. She just watched. Her grandma came out and tried to get her back into her room, but she wouldn't go.

Stubborn as Jules, I thought, and then the reality of it all started to slip in on me. There was no Jules anymore. No dancer girl to laugh with, to plot with, to sit and hold. No more midnight beach trips or shared plans or tears cried on each other's shoulders. I couldn't call her up to talk when I needed her. I couldn't complain about my mom or wonder with her what we were going to do with the rest of our lives.

I heard a loud sobbing, and it took almost a minute to realize the sound was coming from me. I remembered reading that in books — people not being aware of the noises that came from them — and I remembered never believing it. Now I know, I thought. Now I know.

Sandra held me while I cried. Or maybe heaved is a better description, because my whole body was doing it. How can someone hurt this much and live?

The day of the funeral came . . . after forty-eight hours that somehow happened and yet didn't exist. Thousands of people called me, but I didn't listen to their messages on my machine. I sat in my room, and I sat in my car. I went to the dance studio and sat outside on the steps. And I went to Brooke's beach house, climbing over the fence to sit on the deck. I looked for the seagulls dancing, but only one came. She sat and stared at me for the longest time. I stared right back. It wasn't really a seagull — I knew that. It was Jules. Everywhere I went, I could feel her, my One and Only. Everywhere I went, she sat with me.

I guess you could say the funeral was beautiful. The

church was, and the flowers. Everyone came, even Jack. He stood with Rachael off to the side, and they both cried the whole time. Most people did. There was a lot of hugging and holding hands. I sat with the family, all except Rosie, who stayed home with her grandmother. Sandra and I didn't cry at all, but William did, quietly, holding his hands to his face.

A young priest spoke of dying young. Linda read a poem Jules had written long ago about dancing. Someone from school, a girl I didn't know too well, sang "Imagine," by John Lennon, one of Jules's favorite songs. I looked over at Sandra, and we smiled at the lines, at how right it was to hear them with her in church:

> *Imagine there's no heaven, it's easy if you try,*
> *No hell below us, above us only sky.*
> *Imagine all the people livin' for today. . . .*

The casket sat in the front of the church, open to all. I didn't look. Whoever was there wasn't Jules. Jules was at the ocean now, being a seagull. Dancing. And free.